A LAND OF BROKE 'S

Lifepath Adventures: Monks Lifepath Adventures: Monks Lifepath Adventures: Monks Lifepath Adventures: Monks Lifepath Adventures: Monks

STEVE DIXON

First published 2009
ISBN 978 1 84427 371 3

Scripture Union
207-209 Queensway, Bletchley, Milton Keynes, MK2 2EB
Email: info@scriptureunion.org.uk
Website: www.scriptureunion.org.uk

Scripture Union Australia
Locked Bag 2, Central Coast Business Centre, NSW 2252
Website: www.scriptureunion.org.au

Scripture Union USA
PO Box 987, Valley Forge, PA 19482
Website: www.scriptureunion.org

British Library Cataloguing-in-Publication Data.
A catalogue record of this book is available from the British Library.

Printed and bound in India by Thomson Press India Ltd

Cover design: Pink Habano
Internal layout: Author and Publisher Services

Scripture Union is an international Christian charity working with churches in more than 130 countries, providing resources to bring the good news about Jesus Christ to children, young people and families and to encourage them to develop spiritually through the Bible and prayer.

As well as our network of volunteers, staff and associates who run holidays, church-based events and school Christian groups, we produce a wide range of publications and support those who use our resources through training programmes.

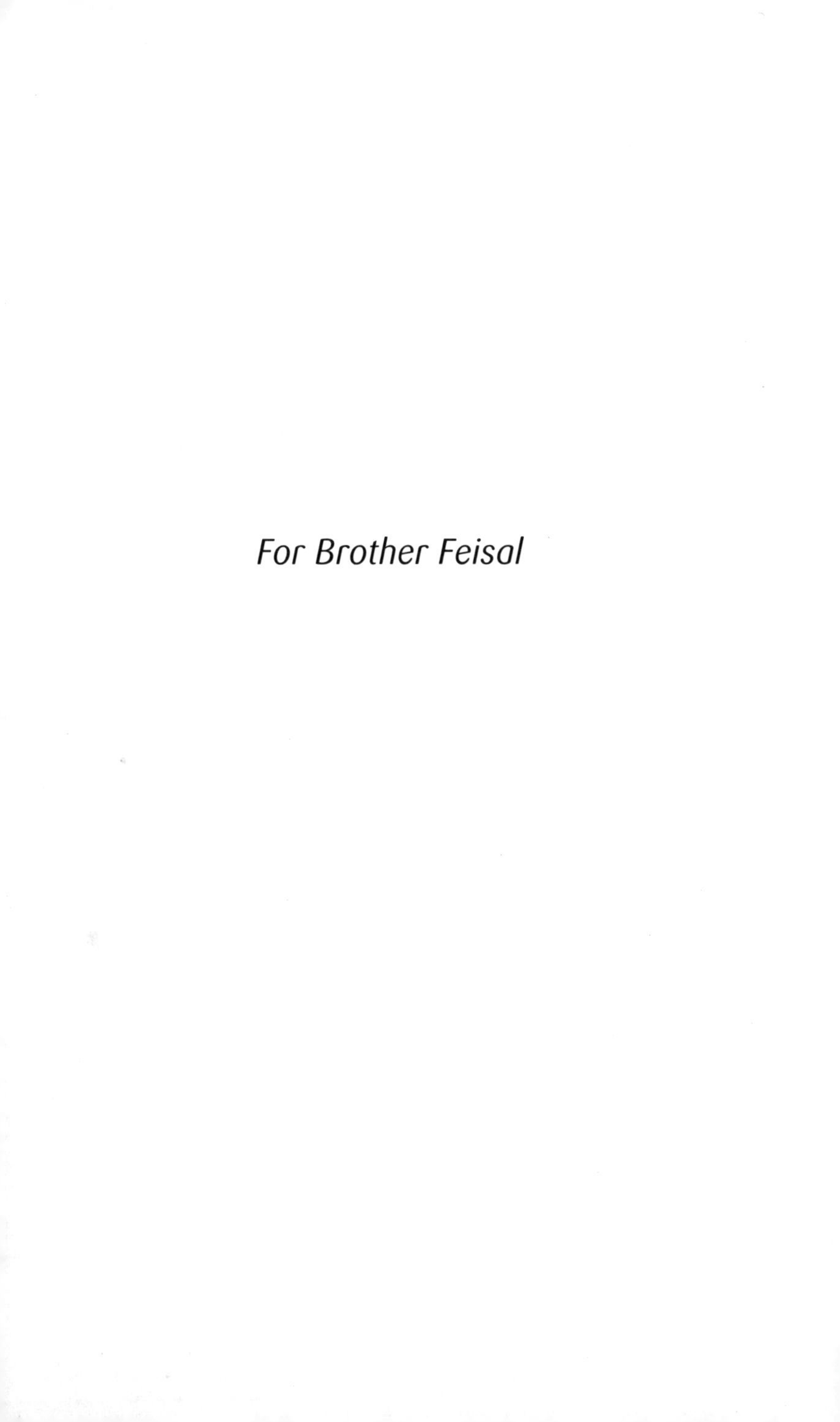

For Brother Feisal

Chapter One

The forest fight

My father promised he would never leave me. That promise is one of the first things I remember. I must have been about 4 years old at the time. I was sitting on his knee by the open fire in the big room of our Hall. I can remember the heat of the fire making my cheeks burn. And I can remember the orange light on the rushes that were spread across the flagstone floor. I'd just asked my father why I didn't have a mother like the village children had and like Siward the boy who served our food. I had a nursemaid, Arlette, but I knew she wasn't my mother. I remember my father being very close, his face very big, but I can't remember what it looked like. All I can remember is the heat and the warm, flickering light. I can't even remember the first things he said; just that somehow he told me my mother had died when I was being born. It's something that happens quite often, I learned as I grew up. I soon found out I wasn't the only motherless child in the world. I think I must have asked my father if he was going to die and leave me, because he held me tight and said, "John, I will never leave you. That's a promise."

I remember those words exactly. And I remember I didn't know what a promise was, but it sounded a strong word the way my father said it. Something about the way my father held me tight, and the warmth and the light made me feel that everything would be all right. Whenever I felt sad or upset in years to come, those words and that scene would rush into my mind to calm me and give me courage. I think I must have been about 5 when I asked Arlette what a promise was. She told me it was something someone said they were going to do.

"And do they do it?" I asked.

"That depends if they're a person who keeps their promises," she told me.

I can remember a few more details about this conversation. We were in a little room at the end of the Hall. There was a tapestry hanging against the stone of one of the walls. It showed riders with spears hunting a stag. I always loved to look at it - at all the details, the tiny forest creatures and the beautiful stag. It was daytime when I asked about promises. It feels like a morning scene in my memory. The sun was bright through the little, high-up window. Arlette had been teaching me my letters and I was making my first words. French words, of course - that was all we spoke in the Hall. I could speak English with the Saxon children from the village, but I don't think they write their language down.

"Is my father a person who keeps his promises?" I asked.

She came and held my face between both her hands.

"Your father is a knight," she said. "Knights must always keep their promises."

* * *

It was seven years since my father made me his promise, and six years since I learned what a promise was. And now my father lay bleeding on the ground, his head in my lap, his breath coming in groaning gasps like someone deep asleep. His eyes were open though. They were staring up into the forest branches that roofed us in, but they looked unfocused, unseeing. I was sure he was dying. Two other men lay dead beside the forest path we had been travelling on. Three knights' horses and my pony shifted about amongst the trees, waiting for someone to take charge of them.

It was supposed to be a great day out – a treat for me. My father and I had been on our way to Baron Gilbert's castle. He was our lord and my father had to serve him in return for the land we had. Every so often Father and all the other knights who owed Baron Gilbert service were called to the castle to a court where they would discuss the affairs of the Baron's estates and settle disputes. Father held a little court in the Moot Hall in our village to sort out affairs in his manor. For the last year or so, he'd let me stand beside his chair so that I could see how things were decided. He'd explained to me that this was how the whole country of England was run – little courts in little halls, and bigger courts in castles, right up to the King, meeting with his great barons. This was how the law and the peace were kept. Or had been in the time of old King Henry – "The Lion of Justice" as they called him. But this was the year of our Lord Jesus 1141, the old king had been dead six years, no one seemed to be sure who was king any more, and my father lay dying in my arms.

I wasn't crying. I must have been in shock. I didn't know what to do. My heart was thumping and my hands felt clumsy. I kept stroking my father's hair as if that would do some good. It was what Arlette did to me when I was ill. He hadn't had his war helmet on when we'd been attacked. It was a warm April day and he hadn't even been wearing his mail coat. We'd been riding happily through the forest pointing out the birds and the squirrels to each other, looking forward to the feast and the entertainment there would be after the court business, when suddenly my father had stopped his horse and listened. Then he'd shouted to me, "Ride on – gallop!" and he'd turned his horse and whisked his sword from its scabbard.

I did as he told me, but a moment later I heard a yell and I pulled my pony up. Swinging round I saw two knights, helmeted and with shield and lance in hand charging towards my father. I was 11 years old and had no weapon. I could do nothing to help and my father had been right to tell me to run. But how can a son run away when his father is about to be killed? I sat on my pony, gripping the reigns and stared. Then, for a moment, I thought perhaps my father wouldn't die. The forest path was narrow and his attackers could only come at him in single file. He had no time to unsling the shield that was hanging across his shoulders but he swung his sword, knocking aside the first man's lance and as the knight rode past my father somehow managed to catch him a blow in the back of the neck, just below his helmet.

He crashed off his horse, hit a tree trunk, fell to the ground and lay still. But the second knight charged in straight behind the first and my father had no time to parry his lance. It caught him in the ribs and sent him, too, tumbling to the forest floor. I shouted out, and maybe that was what gave my father his chance. The knight saw me and charged on down the path in my direction. I should have turned and fled, but I couldn't move. My father had begun to teach me the use of the sword, but even if I'd had one, I would have had no chance against the charge of a grown warrior. If I'd had a weapon that day, I don't think I would even have drawn it. He came so close that I could hear the panting of his horse, but then the man pulled on the reigns and dragged his horse to a halt. He paused for a moment, maybe realising for the first time that I was only a boy, and not worth his trouble. I can remember nothing of his face, just two hard, dark eyes on either side of the nose piece of his helmet. The horse snorted, and the rider swung it round, levelled his lance and charged at my father again. But by then my father had managed to get to his feet and bring his shield round to protect his body. At the last moment, before the man's lance hit his shield, my father stepped to one side. He had been standing with his back to a tree and the man drove his lance straight into it. The shock shattered the weapon and jerked him out of his saddle. He yelled in pain as he landed and before he could struggle to his feet my father was standing over him. They struck each other at the same time. The man, swiping wildly from the ground slashed my father's thigh, but my father's blow was a clean thrust into the neck. He put all his weight behind it and the man's chain mail gave way. He died instantly.

I trotted back to the scene and jumped from my pony, but my relief only lasted a moment. The sword slipped from my father's hand and he tottered towards me as if he were drunk. He was a few paces away when he dropped to his knees and knelt, swaying, with his arms wrapped round his chest. Blood was running down his leg and I could see that it was also oozing out from under the hand he had pressed to his ribs. He looked at me and I think he tried to smile, then he toppled forward. I got down beside him and heaved until I was able to roll him over. His face looked white and as I stroked his hair he started to shake.

I took his head between my hands and turned it so that his glazed eyes were pointing at me then I bent my face down to his and shouted, "Father! Don't leave me! You said you wouldn't! You said you'd never leave me! You promised!" I kept on shouting, "You promised!" over and over, but I was sure it was hopeless. And then something happened to his eyes. They seemed to focus again and I knew that he could see me. He groaned and lifted his hand to hold on to my arm. I stopped shouting and began to cry.

He took three or four gasping breaths, then managed to speak.

"Sit me up, John," he whispered.

I got behind him and managed to lever his shoulders off the ground. I kept on pushing until he was sitting. He lolled forward and it was several moments before he spoke again – a croak that I could only just hear.

"Fetch horse," he said. "Can't walk."

I knew my father's horse well and it came easily to my voice. It stood steadily as my father draped his arms across its back.

"Kneel down - make a back, son," he said. "Have to stand on you."

I did as he told me and my father used me as a mounting block. He groaned and growled as he hauled himself onto the horse's back, but at last he was on, with his head lying on the creature's neck and his arms clasped tight around it.

"Sword and shield," he mumbled.

I fetched them and managed to secure them to my pony's back.

"Lead horse," my father instructed.

"Home?" I asked.

"No - onward," he told me.

So I took the stallion's bridle and led him along the path, away from the scene of the ambush. My pony followed on without trouble. But the knights' horses stayed with their fallen masters.

I'd been to Baron Gilbert's castle before and I knew it was still a long way off. At a normal pace it would take some hours, but creeping along as we were I was sure we wouldn't arrive before nightfall. My father groaned at the slightest jolt and soon he began muttering like a man in a fever. I couldn't see how he would survive. But then the path crossed a stream. I stopped and brought water in my cupped hands. My father managed to suck some of it up and I splashed the rest on his face. Then he made a great effort to speak.

"Path," he croaked, "down."

The pathway to the castle continued across the stream, but I could see there was another, narrower track leading down an incline, following the course of the water.

"Go down," my father repeated.

So I led his horse carefully down the track and my pony followed. Every now and then I would stop for more water, but my father was no longer able to drink so I just used the water to cool him. He was rambling deliriously and I knew I would get no further directions from him. The situation seemed hopeless. There was nothing for it but to keep on following the track and see where it led.

* * *

It led into a valley, and before we got to the bottom, the trees gave way to open hillside. The forest had been cleared and the slopes were dotted with sheep, scores of them. On the common ground at our village we grazed cattle, and everyone kept pigs, but no one had sheep. I stood still for a moment and listened to the occasional baa sound they made. I shut my eyes, exhausted. The sound of the sheep and the stream running down the valley side lulled me and I almost went to sleep on my feet. Then a shout roused me. In the bottom of the valley, the stream joined a little river, and on the river bank a man was standing, waving his arms. He seemed to have some kind of black apron hanging down his front, but the rest of him was covered in a long, wide-sleeved robe that shone white in the afternoon sun.

I had no idea who or what he was, but he was another human being, and he had shouted in French. Perhaps he could give help. I bent close to my father's face and whispered to him, "I've found someone. It's going to be all right. Don't give up. Remember your promise."

He was still murmuring, so I knew I hadn't lost him yet, but his arms were slack around the horse's neck. I had to hold him on as we crept carefully downwards. The man in white could obviously see the difficulty. He hitched his robe up, showing bare legs above his stockings, and began to run up the slope.

"Dear God in heaven preserve you!" he said when he reached us and saw the state my father was in. "Come on – there's no time to lose."

Then he heaved his robe up still further, showing that he wore absolutely nothing underneath, and to my amazement he sprang onto the horse's back behind my father. He took the reins in one hand and passed the other arm round my father's waist, hauling his body upright. The sleeve of the man's robe fell back to show a massive forearm, bulging with muscle.

"Follow me, boy," he shouted, "and be quick about it."

Then without waiting for an answer he rode off at a smart trot, my father jiggling in front of him like a child's doll. As he rode down the hill I noticed that the top of his head was completely shaved. The only hair he had was in a neat band running all around his head like a crown.

I had to hang my father's shield on my back and lay his sword across my lap so that I could sit on my pony. I must have looked a strange warrior, dwarfed by his arms, as I trotted after the man who'd taken my father. There was a bend in the valley and the man in white had disappeared round it before I caught up. I wondered where he could be leading me. Some peasant's hovel no doubt. But at least it would be somewhere for my father to rest. If he could rest and we could bandage his wounds and he could survive his fever perhaps there was hope. But the wound to his chest was serious, and even the cut on his thigh could be fatal. I knew strong men in our village who had died from the simplest of injuries - a cut from a clumsy stroke with a scythe at corn harvest could cost a life if the wound went bad. I had small hope that a peasant too poor to afford breeches would have any medicines to deal with my father's wounds.

Then I rode round the bend and saw what was at the end of the valley. First there was a level area laid out in fields. Further on were a few buildings, then a wooden boundary wall and inside that I could see the roofs of many more buildings. One stood out above all the others. It had a tall, pitched roof, like a lord's hall, and a stout square tower like something from a castle. The man in white was racing on towards a gateway in the wall and shouting, but I was too far away to hear what he said. I saw another white-robed figure pull the gates open, then I noticed they were dotted all over the place, like seagulls in a field.

As I came close to the gate, I called out to one of the men who was clearing brambles beside the path. He stared at me, an 11-year-old boy, weighed down by a shield and a warrior's sword, with as much amazement as I was staring at him.

"What is this place?" I shouted.

In my haste, I'd spoken in French and I realised that if he was working on the land he was probably Saxon, but he replied in my own language without hesitation, and in an accent more cultured than my own.

"This is the Abbey of St Mary," he told me. "St Mary in the Wilds."

Chapter Two

Brother Peter

By the time I got through the gateway, the man who'd taken my father was there to meet me. I might not have recognised him among the other men who were hurrying towards me since they all wore the same uniform - a white robe and a black tabard, like an apron. But one thing marked out our rescuer - he was covered in blood. And I recognised something in the way he moved - muscular and forceful, as if he were used to decisive action and taking command. He strode up to my pony and lifted me clean out of the saddle, shield, sword and all, with no more effort than if he'd been lifting a puppy.

"Your father?" he asked.

I nodded.

He took my father's sword from me and held it for a moment, weighing it and feeling the balance, then he passed it quickly to one of the other men who had gathered round us. Someone else lifted the shield from my shoulders.

"Don't worry, boy," the man told me. "The gear will be well looked after, until your father can use it again."

"Will he live?" I asked. My voice felt very light and shaky.

The man knelt down in front of me and took my shoulders in his hands. The power, just in that light grip, surprised me. It made me feel safe.

"What's your father's name?" he asked.

"Henry," I told him, "after the old king."

"Sir Henry? Sir Henry Fitzherbert?"

"You know my father?"

The man looked up at the other white-robed figures who had gathered round us.

"Brother William, tell the Abbot and Father Prior that we have one of our patrons in the Infirmary," he instructed. "Brother Thomas, go to the Infirmary at once and tell the Infirmarer who he has in his care. The rest of you, get about your business. I'll attend to this young man."

His face was round and tanned, with small pale blue eyes. They were surrounded by the kind of wrinkles that come from frequent smiling. But it was a serious face, and his eyes seemed very serious and powerful as they looked into mine.

"I'm Brother Peter," he said. "And you are?"

"John," I told him. "Sir, will my father live?" I asked again.

"I thank you for your courtesy," he replied, "but you need not call me 'sir' - if you would call me 'brother' I should be honoured."

He took my hand and led me to a stretch of rough grass inside the fence, then sat down. He patted the grass next to him and I sat at his side. A warm, sweaty smell came from him - like the smell the peasants have in our village when they've been working in the fields. It was mixed with the smell of earth and corn - a good, healthy smell.

"Our Infirmarer is a skilled physician," he said. "Your father would have no better treatment anywhere else in the kingdom, rest assured of that."

"I want to see him," I said, and I started to get up. But he put a heavy hand on my shoulder.

"In a little while, John," he said. "When he's been treated, they'll send for you. If you went now, you'd just be in the way. You should rest. Are you hurt yourself?"

I told him that I wasn't - only tired. The blood that covered my tunic was all my father's.

"Tell me what happened," Brother Peter said. "Your father has been wounded in combat - by sword and lance I should say. Has the war come this far into the wilderness?"

I told him what I could, but everything had happened so quickly that there seemed little to tell. I had no idea who our attackers had been or whether we'd been caught up in the war. My father had told me that there was fighting in different parts of England to do with who was to be ruler, but he had never said that it was anywhere near our land.

"So there are two dead men in the forest," Brother Peter said. "We will send some of our lay brothers to collect their bodies. They must at least have Christian burial, whoever they are. And Baron Gilbert must be informed of this bloodshed in his land."

A bell sounded and soon a steady stream of white-robed figures was passing through the gates from the fields and across the open ground between the outer enclosure wall and the collection of buildings that seemed to make up this strange community.

"That's what I should be doing," Brother Peter told me.

"Where are they going?" I asked.

"To church."

I knew what a church was. We had one in our village – a rough little stone hall with a table at the end where the priest acted out the last meal of our Lord Jesus. I looked at the cluster of buildings.

"There's a church in there?" I said.

Brother Peter laughed: a big sharp sound like a shout. It startled me. Then he pointed to the tower that rose above all the other buildings, and the steeply sloping roof that ran from it.

"That's the church, John!" he said.

"But it's huge!" I replied. "Ours is nothing like that big. I thought it was some kind of castle with a tower like that."

Brother Peter laughed again.

"God's castle, maybe," he said. "There's some kind of battle going on here, that's for sure. Some kind of siege. Something being defended. But exactly where the enemy is - that's another matter. It's not quite as simple as killing two knights in the forest."

"Are you going?" I asked, pointing to the last few white-robed figures, disappearing through a doorway into the complex of buildings.

"No, no," he said. "I'm excused - thanks to you. I've been ordered to look after you instead."

"Ordered?"

"We're all under orders here, John. Are you hungry?"

I felt as if I ought to be hungry. I'd no idea what time it was or how long since I'd last eaten. But I just felt numb. Normal feelings like hunger didn't seem to be working anymore.

Brother Peter took my hand again and I noticed how rough and hard it felt.

"Come on," he said, pulling me to me feet. "I'll take you to the Guest House. You need to wash. And I need to leave you in someone else's care for a while and get changed." He pointed to the blood that was now dry on his robe. "We'll get you some food and drink. Maybe you'll eat. Maybe you'll sleep. Then maybe your father will be bandaged up and you can go and see him."

Just outside the boundary wall was a stone building, about the size of my father's Hall. Peter led me in through a heavy wooden door. The small, high windows only let in a little light but I could see the room was completely plain. There were no wall hangings like the lovely hunting tapestry at home, and the only furniture was a simple wooden table and a bench. The floor was bare stone, but cleanly swept.

"Is this the Guest House?" I asked, and my tone of voice must have given away my opinion of it.

"You'll find us very plain here, John," Brother Peter said. "Plain rooms, plain food, plain dress. Just wait a moment please."

He went through a door at the end of the room. And for the first time since the horror of the forest fight I was completely alone. I sat on the wooden bench and stared at the wall, following the irregular patterns of bumps and hollows on the stone with my eyes. My mind felt dull and empty. I gradually sensed the thick silence of the place and realised that no one was shouting or even talking anywhere within earshot. In my father's Hall, at Baron Gilbert's castle, out in the village fields, anywhere I'd ever been where there were other people you could always hear voices talking, calling, shouting, laughing –

but here there was nothing. I supposed that Brother Peter had gone to get me some food - at home my father would simply have yelled and Siward would have come running, but here Brother Peter had gone in silence to attend to the task. Silence and birdsong: as my ears started to hunger for sound I could make out the song of nature - nothing could stop that. And there was another sound too, I realised - muffled by distance. It was some kind of singing.

Brother Peter came back with a wooden board on which were a loaf of brown bread and some cheese, a knife, and a pottery drinking cup. I realised that whether I was hungry or not, I was certainly thirsty. I drank deeply from the cup. It was watered down beer.

"What's that singing?" I asked.

He stood still for a moment. A smile spread over his face and he started to hum in tune with the distant song.

"That's what I should be joining in with," he said. "It's the choir monks singing the office. They're singing the office for the ninth hour."

"What is this place?" I asked. "What's it for?"

Brother Peter gave another of those startling shouts that were his way of laughing.

"What's it for?" he repeated. "An excellent question, John. It's for prayer and the singing of God's praise. And it's for serving God's people - the sick like your father, and the poor. And for hospitality. But mostly it's for prayer and praise." He thought for a moment. "Do you know what a mill is, John? Do you have one in your village?"

I told him that we did - a noisy rattling place, down by the river, full of flour dust.

"A mill's a house full of machinery for grinding out flour," Brother Peter said, "and you are now in a monastery, which is a house for grinding out prayer and praise. Bread feeds the body, prayer feeds the soul, and both are needed for the health of God's people."

We listened to the distant song, and Brother Peter began humming again, then he started to sing softly. He had a deep, rumbling voice that actually made me think of the machinery in our mill.

"You're singing in Latin," I said.

"Of course."

"But you speak French. You spoke to the other 'brothers' - is that what you call them? - in French."

"Most of us are from France," he told me. "Our order is from Cîteaux in Burgundy - 'Cistercium' in Latin. People call us Cistercians because of it."

"Then what are you doing here in England?"

"We seek out the wild places of the earth," Brother Peter explained. "Far away places - away from the world, where no one knows we're there except God."

"My father knows you're here," I said, remembering again the horrors of our journey through the forest, and my father's muttered instructions to follow the path down to this hidden valley.

"Ah yes," Brother Peter replied. "Your father knows because he has been generous with his money. He has given us money to help build here. We started off with wooden buildings - timber hacked from the forest - but thanks to your father and other faithful knights of the shire we now have money for stone as you can see. There is much building at St Mary in the Wilds at the moment. Your father gave money, and Baron Gilbert gave us the land."

"Why did the Baron do that?"

Brother Peter smiled and looked at the floor for a moment.

"In Christian charity I should say he gave it from the goodness of his heart," he replied. "But in Christian honesty I have to say I suspect he gave it to God in the hope that no one else should have it."

"What do you mean?" I asked.

"These are dangerous times, John," he told me. "This war is supposed to be about who rules England, but many barons are simply using it as an excuse to settle old scores. So far we've been spared in this shire, but there may come a day when Baron Gilbert has to defend his land against his enemies. He hopes this valley is safe - perhaps we've not yet reached such depths of anarchy that anyone would steal what's been given to God."

He pushed the wooden board close to me on the table.

"Eat, drink," he said. "Look after your body. Then we'll look to matters of the spirit - when I've changed we can pray for your father."

Once I started to eat, I found that I was starving. I ate all the bread and cheese and drank all the beer in no time. Another brother came to see me after a while and brought a second helping and another cup of weak beer. When I'd finished that, he showed me to a small chamber at the end of the room where there was a simple wooden bed and a mattress filled with hay. A clean tunic and breeches were laid out on it and there was a jug of water and a bowl on a table. My clothes were stiff with caked blood, but I managed to get them off and wash myself. Then I put the clean clothes on and lay down on the mattress. I longed to see my father, and the memories of the fight seemed to threaten me with nightmares, but in moments I fell into a deep sleep, untroubled by dreams of any kind.

When I woke, Brother Peter was kneeling on the floor by the door.

"What are you doing?" I asked.

"Praying," he said, "for your father and for you."

He got up in one movement. He was a big man, and I was surprised he could move with such ease.

"Come on," he said. "Now we're both changed and decent, let's go and pray together for your father. There's a chapel in the Infirmary - we can use that."

I got up and followed, but as we left the building I started to lag behind. After a moment Brother Peter noticed.

"What's the matter?" he asked.

"I don't know how to pray," I explained.

Brother Peter looked puzzled. "You go to church?" he said.

"Yes," I told him.

"Don't you pray there?"

"We listen."

"Well, don't you know any of the prayers the priest says?"

"He speaks in Latin," I explained. "I don't know any Latin. Anyway, he's just an old Saxon who mumbles and mutters like a madman. Everyone keeps away from him in the village. I don't think even you'd be able to make out what he said."

Brother Peter knelt down in front of me and looked me in the eye.

"Do you want your father to live?" he asked.

"Of course!"

"Then say, 'God - I want my father to live!' That'll do well enough for a prayer."

"But I can't say it in Latin."

"Say it in French! Say it in Saxon! It's all the same to God!"

This was a new idea to me. I'd always thought that praying was some magic that had to have a special language, like spells.

"Will it work?" I asked.

Peter kept looking straight into my eyes.

"If it were that simple," he said, "no one would ever suffer or die, John. All I can tell you is it helps. I don't know how or why, or what's going to happen to your father, but I can tell you that once the Infirmarer has attended to him, the best thing both of us can do for your father is to pray for him. Prayer and poultices, that's the way to proceed."

He led me towards the Infirmary, at the other side of the compound, but as we approached it, a brother came hurrying out and seeing us he came up to Brother Peter. He whispered to him, then scurried away again.

"The Infirmarer's finished his work for today," Brother Peter explained. "The Abbot suggests that you go and spend some time at your father's bedside now. So it looks as if you're excused chapel! I'll go and do the praying for both of us - in all the languages I know, for good measure. You go to your father."

He showed me into a long room with beds down each side. Several were occupied and he led me to where my father lay, saying he'd call back when it was time to sleep.

My father was lying under a woollen blanket, but there was no blood on it, so I knew that his wounds must have been well bound and the bleeding staunched. He was asleep, but his breathing was even. The light was dim in the room and I couldn't tell how pale he was, but he looked peaceful, and handsome. My heart filled up with love and fear for my father. And fear for myself. Before I knew it, I found myself on my knees beside his bed. One of my father's hands lay outside the bed cover and I held it tight. It was very hot and damp. Tears ran down my cheeks, but I wasn't sobbing, instead I whispered in my homely French, "Dear God, help my father to keep his promise."

I stayed like that for a long time, even though my knees were hurting, and eventually I bowed my head, resting it against the mattress. I was glad that Brother Peter was looking after me, but I still felt very lonely and homesick. I longed for Arlette to put her arm round me and speak some soft, soothing words. I started to drift off into a dream of our Hall, and Arlette stroking my hair. And then I jerked awake with a sudden realisation. It struck me as the strangest of all the strange things about this place that father and I had come to. It was named after a woman, St Mary, but there didn't seem to be a single woman in the place - not in the fields, not bringing the food - no serving wench or wife. It was Father Prior and brother everyone else, but of mothers and sisters there had been no mention at all.

Chapter Three

Called to war

In the week that followed, I found that what I had suspected was true. There were no women in this community at all. There were young men and old men, bearded men (called lay brothers) and clean-shaven men (called monks) but no women. When I asked Brother Peter about it he said, "It just makes things easier." Then he smiled and added, "That's the theory, anyway." He told me there were communities for women too, called convents, where they could be together without men and concentrate on serving God. He told me about the life the monks lived at St Mary's Abbey - the daily balance between work, study, and prayer - and I soon got used to the monks filing in and out of the church for the services, seven times in the day time. They even went once every night, but I never saw that - Brother Peter just told me about it. He explained that it all came from a song called a psalm in the Holy Bible. One bit of the psalm said "Seven times a day I praise you" (meaning God) and another part of it said "At midnight I rise to praise you". So that's what monks had decided to do. They'd been doing it for about 600 years, since a man called Benedict had made a book of rules for them. They still followed those rules all this time later. Brother Peter explained to me that the monks had to go to a room called the Chapter House every morning where they would listen to a chapter of this rule book being read out, just so they didn't forget it.

Brother Peter spent quite some time with me during that first week. I wasn't expected to join in with the praying and singing and studying but he showed me round all the farm buildings and workshops they had and let me try some of the jobs. There was a blacksmith's forge for their tools, a mill for flour to make the bread they all ate and a granary to keep the corn before it went to the mill. There was even a brew house for beer, although the monks only drank it watered down like the beer I'd been given when I arrived.

Brother Peter said all this work was part of being a monk. Benedict had wanted monks to be able to grow their own food, make their own clothes and have enough over to be generous to guests and to poor people. He showed me the wool store where they kept the wool from the sheep that they didn't need for weaving their own clothes. Brother Peter told me they sold the extra wool to help pay for the monastery and to give money to the poor. There was lots of wool, so they must have had plenty of money to give away. The monks didn't like to waste things - they even used the skin of the sheep.

Brother Peter explained how it was made into thin sheets called vellum for the monks to write on. Making the vellum was done in a place called the tannery. It stank so we didn't spend very long looking in there.

Brother Peter took me to look at things to give me some fresh air and something to do, but I spent a lot of that week with my father, bringing him his food and drink and being his nurse. A couple of days after we'd arrived it was obvious he was getting better. The Infirmarer had herbs and ointments that took away his pain and fever and made the wounds start to heal, and soon he was able to talk to me and to the monks. Brother Peter had been asked to make me feel at home, but there was another monk, Brother Alan, who was called the Guest Master and he was supposed to make sure my father had everything he needed. Soon my father was asking Brother Alan to send messages to Baron Gilbert to explain his absence and report the deaths, and to his bailiff at our village to let him know what had happened. Brother Alan explained that the monks did not like to leave their monastery, but there was building work going on, as Brother Peter had told me, so masons and other workmen and suppliers were often going to and fro with materials. My father agreed to pay some of these men to take messages to our village and to the Castle. Brother Alan sent one of the young monks to write the messages down. My father's bailiff couldn't read, but the messenger was told to give his vellum scroll to Arlette.

Two days later I was helping my father to eat his meat broth - a luxury for invalids only, so Brother Peter told me - when the young monk came in carrying a scroll with Baron Gilbert's seal fixed to it. My father showed the seal to me. It was a thick, dark red blob and looked like a big scab, but the important thing about it was the image that was pressed into it.

"Baron Gilbert has a metal stamp with that picture on it," my father explained. "When the wax is still soft he presses the stamp onto it and it makes the picture. Then you know the document has his authority. Look closely, then you'll be able to recognise it if you ever get any letters from Baron Gilbert yourself."

I looked. There were some words in a circle round the outside of the picture, but I couldn't read them. I suppose they might have been Latin. The picture itself showed a man on a horse waving a sword.

My father cracked the seal, unrolled the vellum sheet and started to read. He wasn't a very good reader and it took him a while. I also got the impression that he didn't like what he was reading. His forehead was creased and once he put the sheet down, closed his eyes and sighed.

"Are you alright, Father?" I asked. But he just grunted and went on reading.

At last, he put the vellum down and looked at me hard. It was a strange look and made me feel uncomfortable. It didn't frighten me. It was simply not the way I was used to my father looking at me and I didn't know how to react. My father and I had always been very close. Maybe it was because I didn't have a mother and he'd never taken another wife, but it felt more as if we were companions than father and son. But now he seemed to put a distance between us; he seemed to be trying to stand back from me to weigh me up, to make some decision.

At last he sighed again and looked away from me. He had a fine face, so unlike Brother Peter's round pudding with its big lump of a nose. My father's nose was thin and fine, his brow narrow, and his deep brown eyes always seemed thoughtful even when he was smiling. Now they looked very troubled.

"This is bad news, John," he said, touching the scroll. "The King has been defeated. The Empress has him captive. It seems he was taken in battle at Lincoln two months ago, and now she has him imprisoned in Bristol. This was the reason Baron Gilbert summoned me. In time of war the King may call for his great men to bring their knights to serve in his army. The King's wife has sent word that the duke of our shire must come to London with all his forces. She is raising a new army to fight for the King. The Duke has ordered all his barons to bring their knights to him, and Gilbert is one of his barons. So, Baron Gilbert has commanded his knights to bring all their men to his castle in a fortnight, armed for battle." He picked up the scroll and waved it at me. "I am one of Baron Gilbert's knights," he said, "so these are my orders to join him and fight for the King."

"But Father, you're wounded," I cried out. "You can't go."

He heaved himself up in the bed and winced.

"A fortnight," he said. "I will be well on the mend in a fortnight."

"But you'll still be weak. Surely you can wait."

He smiled at me then and took my hands in his. They were strong hands - every bit as strong as Brother Peter's, but nothing like as big and hard.

"You're right, John, of course - I'll not be at my best. But it could be weeks before we come to battle, maybe months. I'll be strong enough by then. It will be safer for me to ride with the army than to come on later on my own. We've already seen what can happen to a knight riding alone now, even here. It seems that we can avoid this war no longer."

"But why do you have to go at all?"

A week ago - before we'd been attacked in the forest - I might well have thought that my father going off to war was an exciting thing. But now I had seen what fighting really meant, the thought horrified me. As far as I was concerned, those few minutes of panic and bloodshed were enough action for us both for a lifetime.

"It's a debt, John," my father explained - "a promise. In return for our lands, I've promised to serve Baron Gilbert whenever he needs me. In return for his lands, Baron Gilbert has promised to serve the Duke. In return for his lands the Duke has promised to serve the King. And the King promises to protect the rule of law in the country so that we can all enjoy our lands in peace. We are all bound to each other by promises, for the good of all."

"But you promised never to leave me," I said.

I said it quietly, and felt almost embarrassed to mention it. He seemed so troubled already that I didn't want to add to his burdens.

"I won't leave you, John. Don't worry," he said. "Knights don't often die in battle. A knight's worth more alive for ransom than dead on the battlefield. It's the poor peasants that suffer. Think about them. I must bring men from our fields to fight with whatever weapons we can find them. They owe me service for the scrap of land they farm. Siward's father must come, and he may well die in this madness, and Siward's uncle and his elder brother. Worry for them John, but not for me."

I could see that he was tired out by our conversation, and I left him to rest.

There is a covered walkway along the side of the Infirmary building, with benches against the wall, and I was sitting there listening to the birds and the distant crack of a mason's mallet when Brother Peter found me.

"You look glum," he said. "Is your father unwell?"

"He's fine," I replied. "Just tired."

"So what's the matter?"

I wondered whether I should be discussing my father's business, but I didn't suppose that the message he'd received was a secret. In a fortnight, the whole shire would know what was happening.

"Baron Gilbert's called for him to join his army," I told him. "They're going to fight for the King."

"Ah," was all that Brother Peter said.

Absent-mindedly, he gathered the black working apron that hung in front of his robe and swung it backwards and forwards. I'd learned that the apron was called a scapular because it hung from straps over the shoulders. Scapula is Latin for shoulder. That might have been the first Latin word Brother Peter ever taught me. I'd been asking a lot of questions during the last few days, and he seemed to enjoy answering them. The robe, he'd told me, was called a habit. Brother Peter's was very ragged and worn – all the brothers' habits were the same. I'd have been ashamed to walk around in something so frayed and patched.

As we sat together on the bench in the sun, I realised I was paying close attention to the ragged hem of Brother Peter's habit because I didn't want to think about what my father had told me. But I knew I'd have to face it. I was confused as to what was going on, who the King was now that old King Henry was gone and who this Empress was who seemed to have captured the new King.

"Brother Peter," I asked at last, "do you know what this war's about? Can you explain it to me?"

He leaned back against the Infirmary wall and stopped swinging his scapular.

"Well, John," he said, "I can tell you what's happened and what is happening, but whether that will explain things is another matter."

"My father called the war 'madness'," I said.

"Your father is a wise man," the monk replied, and that made me feel good.

"Tell me, then," I insisted.

"Are you patient, John," he said, "because this is rather complicated."

I told him I was.

"Very well then," he went on, "let me try and tell this as a story."

I settled myself against the wall, and he began.

"Once upon a time, all was well in the land of England. King Henry, 'The Lion of Justice', ruled the country well, as he did his land of Normandy in France. He had a son called William, whom he loved dearly, and who was going to be king of England after him. Prince William was a fine young man and a warrior. At the age of 17 he fought beside his father, King Henry, in a battle against the King of France to defend their land of Normandy."

"My grandfather fought with King Henry in France!" I said.

"Well, John, your grandfather and Prince William might well have fought side by side."

"Did they win?" I asked.

"They did, boy, and the Prince celebrated the victory with plenty of wine. Too much wine, it seems. King Henry set sail for England, but his son Prince William stayed behind, drinking with his friends. His father had provided a fine vessel called the White Ship for the Prince to return in, so William took his friends on board and they continued the celebrations for hours, moored in the harbour. The Prince was a royal star and he was surrounded by a sparkling set of nobles – all the smartest young people. When they finally set out for England, night had fallen and they were all very drunk. William was in high spirits and was determined to catch his father up, so he ordered the captain to follow the King at full speed. He did, but he was as drunk as his passengers and in the darkness he ran the White Ship onto a rock. It capsized, sinking rapidly and every one of those young lords and ladies drowned, including the Prince. They say that King Henry never smiled again.

"But, whether he smiled or not, the King had to pull himself together and decide who should rule England when he was dead. He had no more male heirs, but he had a daughter called Matilda. When she was very young she had been married to the Holy Roman Emperor, and so she was known as the Empress - which is helpful, because so many other royal ladies are called Matilda. If we call her the Empress, we won't mix her up with the others. A few years after Prince William drowned in The White Ship Disaster, Empress Matilda's husband died too and she came back to England. Her father, old King Henry, decided that as he had no male heir, she should rule England after him and so he got all the great men of the Kingdom to promise that they would accept her as their sovereign when he was dead. He made them promise again a few years later, just to make sure and all seemed to be well. She got married again, to the Count of Anjou, and that seemed to be good as most of the great men of England were Normans, and the Normans had always been enemies of the people from Anjou. If the new ruler of England was married to the Count of Anjou, King Henry hoped it would stop the Normans and the people of Anjou being enemies.

"When her father, King Henry, eventually died Empress Matilda was in France. She had to go to England to be crowned as the new ruler, but before she could set out, someone else got there before her. King Henry had a favourite nephew called Stephen. He was the Count of Blois, in France. All the other great men in England liked Stephen too - he was a brave warrior and a charming nobleman. When the great men heard King Henry had died, they decided they didn't want a woman to rule over them, and they also didn't like the fact that she was married to the Count of Anjou. So when Stephen decided to try his luck and seize the crown, all the great men broke their promises about serving Matilda and accepted him as King. He was crowned only a month after King Henry had died, while the Empress was still in France. Of all the people who broke their promise the day they bowed down to Stephen as King, the greatest promise-breaker was Stephen himself. He'd been the first of all the nobles to swear that he would accept his cousin Matilda as his sovereign.

"Empress Matilda bided her time. Stephen may have been brave and fashionable, but he was not a great ruler. It didn't take him long to make enemies amongst the barons, and after three years some of the great men were beginning to grumble that they might have been better off with Matilda after all. There were uprisings. The King of Scotland invaded the North of England in support of Matilda. The Welsh began to cause trouble. Then the Empress Matilda herself landed in England with a small army, joined forces with her half-brother, Earl Robert of Gloucester, and together they made war on King Stephen.

"That was two years ago, and now the Empress has captured the King and she has been proclaimed Lady of the English. So whether she rules England or her cousin Stephen does, who can tell. And which duke or baron is on whose side no one can tell from one month to the next either. Now that the great men have broken their promises to the old King it seems that no one's word is worth anything anymore. The dukes and barons change sides as easily as a change in the wind. Your father will ride off to fight for King Stephen, but who is to say he won't find the Duke leads him away to fight for the Empress before the month is out?"

Brother Peter's face had gone a deeper red as he told his story, and he was now slapping his scapular against his leg in an agitated manner. As I watched him, something suddenly struck me as rather strange in the situation.

"You seem to know a lot about all this for someone who lives so far away from the world," I said.

Brother Peter stopped flapping his scapular and looked at me hard.

"I have an interest in such things," he said.

Chapter Four

My new home

The fortnight was nearly up. Messages had been sent back to our village for those men who owed my father service to arm themselves as best they could and meet him at Baron Gilbert's castle. And my father, although he was still weak, was ready to ride. He had moved out of the Infirmary and had been recovering in the Guest House for some days, taking short walks around the garden to build up his strength. I would often walk with him so that he could lean on my shoulder if he needed to, and we were walking there on the morning he was due to leave. Like everything at St Mary's, the garden wasn't for show - it was for a purpose. All that grew there were vegetables and herbs, and the mixed scent of the different herbs filled the air. Although I was still worried that my father was going off to war, it made me feel good to see him so much better. He didn't lean on me once as we walked, and his voice was strong again and businesslike as he described the instructions he'd sent to the bailiff for maintaining the land when so many of the men were away.

"It won't be easy, John," he said. "Much of it will have to lie fallow, so there will be less food. But then there will be fewer mouths to feed without the men. There will be hunger, you can be sure of it. But if it gets to be too much to bear, the bailiff has order to send word here to St Mary's – the brothers will provide for the starving. My greatest fear is that some armed band might sweep through the shire, stealing all the food and animals and burning what they can't take. It seems that the two men who attacked us were stragglers from some renegade war band that had wandered into our lands. They may be the first of many."

"Were they on the side of the Empress?" I asked.

"They were on no side but their own I should think, John. The land is lawless – this war is turning into no more than an excuse for robbery. That's what happens when promises are broken and there is no trust any more."

"But the promises were made to the Empress," I said. "And you are going to fight against her!"

My father stopped and looked in my face with a little smile on his lips.

"I'm impressed by your knowledge, son," he said.

I smiled back.

"Brother Peter has been explaining," I told him.

"He's a good man," my father said. "Do you like him?"

I hadn't really thought about it. I'd been too worried and confused to have any space in my feelings for anyone apart from my father. But now that the question had been asked, I supposed I did.

"He's been kind," I said. "I've enjoyed looking at things with him and talking with him."

"Good," my father said. I thought he was going to say something more, but he just said, "Good," again, rather more forcefully, then went on walking.

I was still puzzled. "Father," I persisted, "why are you going to fight for King Stephen when all the promises were made to Empress Matilda?"

We walked on silently and I thought that for once my father had no answer.

"I know, John," he said at last. "It hurts me. But it would hurt me more to break my own promise. I must follow Baron Gilbert. The only promise I have ever made is to him."

"And to me," I said, quickly.

He looked down and put a hand on my shoulder.

"And to you, of course! And I'm going to be true to both my promises. I shall go and help Baron Gilbert establish an unrighteous king upon the throne of England, which at least will bring us peace and some kind of order, and then I shall return to my dear son and teach him how to be a knight and rule justly over the little parcel of land that God has given him."

Father decided to try his strength and we walked out of the Guest House garden, through the gate and down to the river that flowed close to the monastery enclosure. He sighed a couple of times, and I could tell that it was nothing to do with pain or tiredness. It was the sort of sigh I had heard at home when he was with the bailiff, or holding his little court in the Moot Hall trying to sort out some difficult village problem. We stood by the fast-flowing water and Father stared at it for some time.

"You remember the old story I've told you sometimes about the beginning of things and God's paradise and the first people," he said. "Remember what the story said. Those first people let God down. They took fruit they were told not to take. That story helps me, John, when I think about the world. We all let God down somehow or other in our lives - we're not perfect, and so nothing in our world is perfect. It's not right that Stephen should be King, but it's not right for me to break my oath to Baron Gilbert either. All I can do is do what feels right in my heart and ask God's forgiveness for what wrong might come from it. That's all anyone can do. And God does forgive. That's what our Lord Jesus came to show us - that God forgives." He looked up from the waters and stared down the valley with its sheep and its fields, and the distant bend round which we'd entered the world of St Mary in the Wilds the best part of a month ago. "You should ask Brother Peter to tell you some of God's stories from the Bible," he continued. "He'll know many more than I do. They help you think about the world. Every knight should know them as well as he knows how to use a sword."

I wondered when I would have the opportunity to ask Brother Peter to tell me stories now that we were leaving the monastery.

"How shall I get home, Father?" I asked. "Will you take me before you go to Baron Gilbert, or will the bailiff come for me, or will they let Brother Peter out of the Abbey to take me home?"

My father turned me round to look at the wooden enclosure fence of the monastery with the roofs of its various buildings, and the steep roof and tower of St Mary's church rising above it.

"John, while I'm away," he said, "this is to be your home."

His words were so unexpected that I didn't speak for a moment. Then I began to picture our village and our Hall and I realised how much I had been longing to get back to them. Tears started to prick my eyes.

"Why?" I asked. "This isn't my home! Why do I have to stay here?"

"For safety, John," he told me, gently. "The village isn't safe now - especially with most of the men gone. There are terrible stories about women and children being murdered by the war bands. I can't risk your safety. You must stay here."

"But what about Arlette?"

"I shall send her to Baron Gilbert's castle. As for the peasants, they must do the best they can. If a war band comes they must flee and leave everything to the robbers. It's a terrible thing that the people of England should be reduced to this - hiding in the forests like hunted animals - but that is what they must do."

There was such seriousness in my father's voice I couldn't doubt that what he said was true. I suddenly felt filled with anger. I wanted to see all the great dukes and barons who had plunged us into this mess hung up like murderers from the branches of the forest trees. But the only picture that came to my mind was of our village in flames and the Saxons being chased around the fields by blood-spattered knights who all looked like the man who had charged at me down the woodland path.

"Why can't I go to the castle with Arlette?" I asked.

"Even the castle may be attacked, John," he explained. "A castle under siege is no place for a child."

"But why should the monastery be safe? There are no soldiers to protect us."

"Because God's law rules here," he replied, "and that has not broken down, neither is God's kingship in doubt. We must pray that not even a war band would draw swords against God's army."

"God's army?"

My father pointed to a group of monks, marching out to the fields.

"Men under discipline," he said.

* * *

Early on the morning after my father left, Brother Peter came to find me in the Guest House. I was glad to see his round face and burly frame – he seemed to be the only security left in my world at that moment. But the normally smiling eyes had a worrying seriousness about them as he came towards me. He looked like someone bringing bad news. Surely, my father couldn't be dead already, or our village burned to the ground.

"Congratulations," he said. "You are to join the company of the novices."

"What are they?" I asked.

There was still a lot about St Mary in the Wilds that I didn't understand.

"People training to be monks."

"But I don't want to be a monk!"

For the first time he smiled, probably taken aback by my forcefulness.

"I'm sorry," I said. "I don't mean to be rude. But I don't want to be one of you."

"No," he said, still smiling. "There's no reason you should. But the truth is, John, the Abbot can't think what else to do with you. Some monasteries do have schools for young men like you - but not this one. You are the only child we have." The seriousness came back as he continued. "There's nowhere else to put you, John, and you can't stay any longer in the Guest House. You see, you might be here some time."

"Months?"

"Maybe many months, or longer."

"But my father said he was going to help put an end to the war - so that there would be peace."

"Yes, and Sir Henry and the other knights will do their best. The trouble is that the Earl of Gloucester and all the others fighting for the Empress are doing their best too. And the Empress Matilda is a very stubborn woman. Now she has decided to fight for what her father promised her, it will be very hard to get her to stop. It could take a long time to settle the matter - if it can be settled at all."

"Well if I can't stay in the Guest House, why can't I stay with you?" I asked.

He gave one of his barking laughs at this suggestion, and I must have looked hurt because he quickly controlled himself.

"Of course, boy, that would be wonderful - nothing better. But, you see, I don't have a house here."

"You don't?" I suddenly realised I had no idea where Brother Peter went when he wasn't in church, in the fields, or with me.

"No, not at all. Not even a room to myself. I sleep in the dormitory with the other brothers. The only space I have to call my own is my mattress. And that is all that you will have I'm afraid, John. The novices have a dormitory too, and you will have a bed with them."

"But what will I do all day? Will you still come to see me?"

"No, John, I'm afraid I shan't. It has been quite out of the ordinary for the Abbot to give me so much time to spend with you. Now I must return to my normal routine, and you are to be put in the care of the Master of Novices. There is no expectation that you prepare to take our vows, but it will be for the Master to decide how you spend your time. It might have been possible to put you with the lay brothers - they don't train to become monks either - but I suppose the Abbot must have thought that with the novices at least you would have the Master to watch over you. Perhaps when you are older, if you are still with us, you could join the lay brothers. You could be sent to live at one of our Granges then. The lay brothers look after them for us."

"Granges?"

"Farms belonging to the monastery, a day's ride from the mother house, or thereabouts. We have three, given by Baron Gilbert."

I sat down heavily on my bed. I had a vision of years stretching out ahead of me. Of growing up, growing a beard like the lay brothers I'd had pointed out to me. Growing old and never seeing my father again. Being buried here in an unmarked grave. There was no help for it – I started to cry. I wasn't sobbing and wailing, but my face was soon as wet as if I'd washed it and my breath was coming in gasps. Brother Peter sat beside me and put his big, rough hand on my shoulder. After a moment I put my much smaller and softer hand over his and in some clumsy way we held on to each other.

* * *

Father Jerome, the Master of Novices was a contrast to Brother Peter in every way. Where Peter was bulky and muscular, Jerome was tall, angular and frail; where Peter's face was like some round vegetable – a turnip maybe – Jerome's was like the face of a horse; where Peter's voice was loud and rough, Jerome's was as thin and wavering as the sound of a reed pipe, played badly. But the biggest contrast was age. Although Peter was older than my father, he was still a man in the prime of middle age; but Father Jerome looked old enough to have known our Lord Jesus personally.

When Brother Peter had given me time to get my crying done with and to wash my face, he took me to the Novice House and left me with my new guardian. Father Jerome looked at me with the sweetest smile and his pale blue eyes seemed to shine.

"Welcome, oh welcome Brother John," he said, rubbing his hands together. "Shall I call you Brother? I'm blessed if I know what else to call you if not. We're all brothers after all, are we not - children of the same father."

Mention of fathers was not a good way to start. I wondered what on earth he was talking about, and then I realised he must be talking about God. When I was missing my earthly father so much, there wasn't much room in my thoughts for a heavenly parent.

"Call me what you like," I muttered.

I knew I was being rude, but I hadn't the energy for good manners. I expected a sharp word in reply from the Master and was ready to give back as good as I got. But to my surprise his only reaction was to stop rubbing his hands together.

"Well then," he said, "Brother John it is."

Now he flung his arms out wide and spun round like a dancer.

"Welcome to our world," he said. "It's where we eat and study - and sleep, of course, but we don't do more than is necessary of that. Now, come along and I'll show you your place."

He started backing away from me towards a group of hay-filled mattresses on the floor.

"What's to show?" I said. "They're all the same."

"Even so, even so," he replied, without any hint of offence, "one of them is yours, dear brother. And it is... this one!"

He announced it with triumph, as if it were a great discovery, and patted the rough blanket covering one of the mattresses.

"Come along then, and survey your domain!" he cried.

I slouched towards him. So far, I had worn ordinary clothes - breeches and a jerkin - but on the mattress lay a small version of a novice's habit.

"Well now, I'll wait outside while you change - though privacy is something you must get used to doing without, I fear. And then we will join the other novices in the field."

"What?"

"The others have already been given their work for the morning. We must join them quickly, or it will be time to come back before we've arrived! I have something special for you this morning - not too back-breaking to begin with, or too rough on your hands until they harden."

This seemed like the last straw.

"I am not working in the fields!" I informed him, firmly.

For the first time Father Jerome seemed taken aback, but with genuine surprise, not anger.

"But why ever not, dear brother? Surely it's the most wonderful thing to be out tending God's garden!"

"I am not a peasant!" I snapped. "What do you take me for - some Saxon lout? I'll have you know my great grandfather was a knight of Normandy who fought beside the Conqueror at Hastings. The shield he carried that day still hangs in my father's Hall. My grandfather fought beside King Henry in France. And my father is Sir Henry Fitzherbert, Baron Gilbert's man, who at this very moment is on a mission to save the King of England!"

For the moment, the horrors of the fight in the forest were forgotten and I felt every inch the heir of a line of noble warriors going back to who knows when. My blood was up and I was ready to fight back if the Master took a swipe at me for my cheek. But he did nothing of the kind. Instead, he stretched his arms out towards me.

"My dear, dear brother," he said, "you must be missing your father very much. And you will be so worried for him, of course."

I stared at him in astonishment.

"I have a suggestion to make," the Master went on, softly. "Your family are clearly connected at the highest level and are used to serving persons of no less importance than kings. Would it please you Brother John, to join the service of the highest king of all? Might you wish to be an adviser in the service of the great King of all Kings? Perhaps, when you are changed into his livery, you might like to watch us work today and advise us. I am sure you will have many tips to give us from the way your father organises the farming of his land? We would be honoured to have your counsel."

What surprised me most of all was the Master's use of the word "us". Surely, that couldn't mean what it seemed to mean. But when I had changed into the livery of the King of Kings - my new novice's habit - and allowed the Master to lead me out to the fields, to "watch and advise", I saw that it meant exactly what I had thought. Father Jerome took firm hold of a hoe, bent his back, and for all his age he set about his work with as much vigour as the youngest of his novices.

Chapter Five

A scuffle in paradise

It's very boring watching other people work and doing nothing yourself. It's also hard not to feel guilty. I felt sure that the novices would be looking at me, wondering why I wasn't joining in, having bad thoughts about me, maybe muttering amongst themselves and passing comments, maybe even making some sharp remark to me. To start with, this helped me fight the boredom as I spent time running over in my head the angry replies I'd make if any of these peasant labourers had the cheek to criticise me. But none of them did. In fact, none of them seemed to be at all aware of my presence - not even the Master of Novices. There were no comments about anyone or anything. They worked with concentration and in silence, hoeing and weeding between their crops. I was reduced to having bad-tempered conversations with myself in my head about how ridiculous and unfair it was to expect a person of my background to be out in the fields. But in the end even that diversion petered out and I was left with the task Father Jerome had given me -

to watch the novices at work and advise on improvements. I realised that to supervise in this way was not, perhaps, unfitting for a knight's son. But at the same time, I realised I was unable to do it. I had no idea what were the best ways to farm – I had never taken any interest. My only interest had been in tales of the heroic deeds of my ancestors and the glamour of castles, knights and courts. In this situation, I was useless. My mind emptied, and the boredom really took hold.

Time passed. The sun rose in the sky. Shadows shifted. I became very aware of little details like the movement of shadows. And the movement of beetles. I found myself searching in amongst the roots of grasses to find any little creatures to watch. My love of God's creatures wasn't limited to the birds and the larger wildlife of the forest that my father and I had been enjoying as we'd ridden along the woodland path on that disastrous morning a month ago. I was fascinated by the tiny things, weighed down by their shiny black armour, that marched across the floor of our Hall, or picked their way carefully among the roots and stalks outside. I remember once watching a woodlouse – the simplest of creatures – and thinking that if only a blacksmith could make me a suit of armour with sheets that moved and slid over each other as easily as those of the woodlouse, then I would be invulnerable. I had been sitting under the table at the end of our Hall, where my father and I would eat. I started to think of home – the cool shade in the Hall on a summer's day, the smell of the rushes on the floor, the shouting and laughing in the kitchen as food was being prepared, and the brilliant rectangle of colour and light that was the open doorway on the world – patches of yellow-gold and green and blue, bold as a banner.

I was miles away in these memories when a shout brought me back to the present. My eyes followed the sound and I saw something unexpected – two novices fighting. What struck me as extraordinary was not the fact that they were fighting, but the way they were doing it. They weren't rolling on the ground, kicking and gouging like our village youths when they set about each other; they were standing up like warriors and using their hoes as weapons. And they weren't using them like the quarterstaves our villagers would do battle with when we had games and competitions to celebrate the harvest. They were trying to swing them at each other like battle swords. By the time the Novice Master intervened, one of them had already received a blow to the knee that would have crippled him for life if they really had been using swords. As it was, he was dancing with the pain as he tried to continue defending himself. He was probably relieved when Father Jerome thrust himself between them.

I was astonished at the Novice Master's fearlessness as he stepped into the mêlée, and at his agility as he dodged the sweep of a hoe. But equally astonishing was the speed with which the fight ended. As soon as the two novices saw the Master between them and heard his thin voice cry, "Enough!" they stopped at once and leaned on their hoes panting with their heads bowed. The one with the injured knee was actually using his implement as a crutch, and after a whispered word with both of them, Father Jerome sent this invalid over to me.

He stood in front of me, still staring at the ground, and said, "Father Jerome asks if you would be so kind as to walk with me to the Infirmary to have my knee bandaged, so that I may lean on you if needs be."

"Why don't you use that?" I asked, rather rudely, pointing at his hoe.

"The Master says I must leave it here, to be used for the purpose for which it was intended. And that you are to be my crutch, if you will allow it."

I looked at him closely. He had spoken using French that was more perfect and courtly than my country boy's accent with its mixture of Saxon sounds picked up from Siward and the villagers. It was more refined even than my father's French, or Baron Gilbert's. His head was bowed, but I could see his face was fine - not the face of a labourer. It was pale-skinned, despite the time I assumed he must spend outdoors every day, and his hair - short, but as yet unshaved at the crown - was thin and such a pale blonde that it was almost white. He continued to stand in front of me until I realised that a decision was required of me before he could move.

"All right," I said, getting up.

We walked together to where Father Jerome was waiting and the pale novice handed the Master his hoe.

"Thank you, Brother Simon," he said, and turning to me, "Thank you Brother John. God has clearly provided you for this very duty today."

Brother Simon and I set off for the monastery buildings, but he did not lean on me despite his obvious pain. I could hear him gasping with each step and I started to feel sorry for him.

"It's all right, you know," I said. "I don't mind you using my shoulder if it would make it easier."

I was looking up at him and he glanced at me quickly. It was the first time our eyes had met. His were dark brown - an unexpected contrast to the rest of his colouring - and I could see the pain in them. He seemed a very young man - perhaps only in his twenties.

"Thank you," he said, and he placed his hand on my shoulder with such weight that I could tell how badly he needed the support.

Progress was slow. I'd already learned that conversation was not encouraged in the monastery. The rule was only to speak when necessary for the job in hand. Nonetheless, I couldn't bear to make this long slow shuffle to the Infirmary without passing a word, and I was full of curiosity.

"Where did you learn to fight, like that?" I asked.

Brother Simon seemed surprised. "Like what?" he said.

"You were using your hoe like a sword - as if you knew how to use a sword."

"My father taught me," he replied.

We continued in silence for a while longer. It was clear that he wasn't going to speak unless spoken to.

"What were you fighting about?" I asked at last.

"Brother Hubert insulted our Lady," he said.

"Holy Mary?" I asked, shocked.

"No, no - heaven forbid," he said with a laugh. "Even Brother Hubert wouldn't speak ill of our Lord's mother. No, I meant the Countess Matilda - she that was Empress and is now the Lady of the English."

"What did Brother Hubert say about her?"

"Things that shouldn't be said about any woman," Brother Simon replied, with embarrassment, "and certainly not by a Christian in such a place as this."

I could imagine what he was talking about, but I realised that I probably didn't know the French words for such things. I knew the Saxon well enough.

"But why would he insult her?"

"He thinks it's Lady Matilda who should be locked up in a castle dungeon, not Count Stephen, and that Count Stephen is rightful King of England."

"My father is fighting for King Stephen," I said, quietly. But somehow, loyalty to my father didn't make me want to shake off this invalid supporter of Matilda.

"It's one thing to fight for a king," he said, "It's another thing entirely to insult a lady."

Brother Simon said nothing more, sticking to his rule of speaking only to respond to my questions, so we moved onward in silence.

We had nearly reached the gate to the monastery compound when I asked, "Will you be punished?"

"When I'm bandaged, I must see the Abbot. Brother Hubert will have to see him too. The Abbot will bring the matter before the whole community and then decide on punishment."

"Won't you tell him what happened? It's not fair that you should be punished for defending a lady."

"I'll tell him if he asks, but there's no excuse for what happened, Brother John. I expect to be punished."

"What will happen to you?"

"This is not the first time Brother Hubert has provoked me to blows. In the past, we have been warned in private and rebuked before the community. This time, I expect we will be banned from joining in the church services."

"That sounds like a reward, not a punishment," I said, without thinking.

His brown eyes were very serious and puzzled when he looked at me.

"It's what I've come here to do," he said "To sing God's praises. What could be worse than to be prevented from doing the one thing your heart longs to do? The rest of the punishment is nothing next to that."

"There's more?"

"I expect I'll have to eat alone, and I'll have to lie on the floor at the doorway to church so that the other brothers can step over me when they leave. The Abbot will decide how long Brother Hubert and I will have to continue with our punishments until it is enough."

As I was returning to the fields, after leaving Brother Simon at the Infirmary, that final part of the punishment seemed to me to be the worst. In fact the only part that really was a punishment. Such humiliation was the last thing that anyone of noble blood would be able to tolerate and I couldn't help wondering what kind of a family Simon must come from to be able to accept it.

Before I reached the area that the novices had been working in, I saw Father Jerome leading his little group back towards the monastery. Brother Peter had taught me to pray for my father by showing me that praying was about sharing your feelings with God - so I said a little prayer to God in my head saying thank you that the fight and looking after Brother Simon had used up the last of the time out in the field.

"Brother John," the Novice Master said quietly, as I joined him, "thank you for completing your task so helpfully."

"I got him to the Infirmary," I said. "He'll be going on to see the Abbot."

"Ah yes," said Father Jerome. "I actually meant your other task."

For a moment I didn't understand, but then I remembered I was supposed to be reporting on their work.

"So how did you judge our techniques?" the Master asked. "Would your father be satisfied with us if we were farming his lands?"

I didn't know what to say. I still resented being in this situation and part of me wanted to tell him the novices were no good. But I found it hard to be cross with this smiling old man who could labour like a youth and bring men to order like a lord with a single word. In any case I knew I'd have no reply if he asked me what was wrong with their work.

"My father always likes people who work hard," I said.

"Effort isn't in question, dear brother," the Master replied. "Labour hard, pray hard and study hard - that's our life here. But we must always seek correction in our methods, I feel - in every one of our activities. If anyone can show us a better way, we should be open to it. Don't you agree, Brother John?"

But I wasn't interested in the ways of the monks and how they could be improved. Something much more intriguing was in my thoughts, so I ignored his comments and went straight to the subject that was preoccupying me.

"Brother Simon was telling me something and he mentioned his father," I said. "Do you know who his father is?"

"Ah yes, my young friend. I do indeed."

"What kind of a person is he?"

"I've never met him, my brother, so what kind of a person he is I cannot tell you. But I can tell you his station in life, if that is what you meant. Brother Simon's father is a great noble in France, John - a relative of the Count of Anjou. And the Count, as I'm sure a wise young man like you will know, is the husband of Matilda - whom we are now to call The Lady of the English, I understand."

"That must be why Brother Simon was on Matilda's side in the fight with Brother Hubert."

"Yes," said the Novice Master, sadly, "I suppose it is understandable - but still we should not be doing battle here on behalf of the great ones of this world. Our calling is to fight for our Lord Jesus Christ, and with spiritual weapons, not farmer's tools. Do you know your Bible, John?"

I had to admit that I didn't, beyond the stories that my father and Arlette had told me.

"Ah Brother John, then you are poor indeed. It is a treasure chest full of jewels. Let me show you one."

I was confused and for a moment I really thought he was going to bring some sparkling gem out from under his habit, but instead he stopped and looked at me with shining eyes.

"The prophet Isaiah spoke of a wonderful time when every last sword and weapon would be turned into farmer's tools so that they might bring life and not death to the world. Isn't that a jewel of a hope?"

After my experience of the bloodshed in the forest, I couldn't help but nod.

"And yet here are two of my novices turning hoes into swords in the name of the princes of this world. John, dear John, we cannot be bringing this civil war into paradise."

"Paradise?" I asked.

We were at the gate to the monastery compound and Father Jerome lingered there as the novices went on. He took a deep breath, and the troubled frown left his high forehead as he looked around him - through the gate, to the high-roofed church, and out again to the valley and the fields.

"This is as near paradise as we shall get on this earth, John," he said. "Fresh air, exercise, our own food from the soil, the treasures of our library to rummage in, all brothers and subject to no one but God. What could be better? Let's go and read his Word for a little while, then we will go to church and give thanks to the Lord for his goodness."

Chapter Six

Lessons

Although it was made very clear to everyone that I was not preparing to become a monk, I was still expected to attend the church services – the offices, as they were called. So it was suggested that I learn Latin to help me understand them and to give me something to do during the times set aside for reading and study. I protested, but when Father Jerome pointed out that if I could speak Latin I might become a royal ambassador one day, I grudgingly agreed to try. And I became slightly more enthusiastic when I was told that my teacher was to be Brother Peter. I was lonely without Father and the company of the monk who'd brought us into the monastery seemed to offer at least some faint connection with the world I'd left behind. But the lessons didn't go well. Brother Peter seemed bad-tempered from the outset, as if he didn't want to be teaching any more than I wanted to be studying. So that we wouldn't disturb the novices, we had to study in a dark little hut that had been put up as a store for the builders. Brother Peter seemed far too big for the cramped space, like a bear in a cage, and he snarled like a bear whenever I got things wrong. I became frustrated and angry in return, and as the days dragged on any friendly feelings we might have had for each other seemed gone forever.

However, a new friendship did begin to grow elsewhere. Following my refusal to labour like a peasant Father Jerome didn't insist that I do more than accompany the novices to their place of work. But once, not long after the combat, when Brother Simon was clearly struggling with his injured knee, the Novice Master asked if I wouldn't mind helping the invalid. The task was log-splitting, and I set up the logs and gathered the pieces, while Brother Simon swung the axe. He did it very well and the thump of the blade and flying wood were so exciting that when he offered to show me how to do it I was glad to accept. I reminded myself that Brother Simon was in fact a nobleman, and of a far more noble family than mine, so it could do no harm to my dignity to help him or learn from him.

After that, I often helped Brother Simon, joining in alongside him with whatever duty was set for the day, and the Novice Master allowed us to work together long after Brother Simon's knee was mended and my help was no longer necessary. We did not talk, beyond what was needed for the task, but it's surprising how a friendship can grow through quietly working together – a silently offered hand, implements passed with a smile and a nod. A monk was expected to be able to help with any work in the monastery, so the novices had to learn about every skill. As well as working with me in the fields and garden, Brother Simon took me to learn from the lay-brothers who wove sheep's wool into the cloth for our habits, or worked in the tannery and forge. We cleaned and cooked together in the kitchen and once helped the masons with the building work. The day we helped the masons, I was astonished to see even the Abbot with a mallet and chisel in his hand, squaring off a block of stone.

I had no brother or sister, but as we worked together in the monastery – young and old, noble and peasant, monks, novices, lay brothers and hired hands together – the word "brother" started to have a powerful meaning for me. I began to see what Father Jerome had meant when he'd said this was a glimpse of paradise – all brothers working together under God. There's no better way to describe it than to say that it felt good. It felt right. It felt as if it were the way things are meant to be.

Cistercians are plain in all things, including food. They eat mostly bread, cabbage and beans. But fish is allowed on special occasions. Brother Simon had great skill in fishing, and once, about six weeks after my father's departure, he took me to the pool to show me how it was done. The pair of us were able to spend an afternoon by the gently shifting water, in the bright warmth of an early June sun. It was the first time I'd really had a chance to talk to him without others nearby to shush and tut, and although I knew we were supposed to limit our words to the job in hand I couldn't help asking a question that had continued to trouble me.

"Father Jerome told me that you're related to the Count of Anjou," I said.

"That's right, John," he told me, "although we don't talk of such things here."

"So you're a noble."

"In the eyes of the world."

"Then why do you labour like a peasant?" I asked. "I've agreed to do it because you do," I went on, feeling rather grand in putting it like that, "but I want to know why you do it."

"I'm not the only brother from a noble family, you know," he told me. "Brother Hubert is from one of the leading families of Boulogne and there are many more here."

"But why do you all lower yourselves like this?"

Brother Simon gazed at the point where his line touched the water.

"A knight should serve his lord, shouldn't he?" he said at last.

I agreed.

"And he serves his lord in return for the gift of land."

"That's how my father explained it to me," I replied.

"So who gave this land?" Brother Simon asked.

"Baron Gilbert," I said.

He laughed gently.

"But who gave it to Baron Gilbert?"

"The King?"

"And who to the King?"

I'd never thought about it but I told him I supposed it must be God.

"But I don't understand what that has to do with working like a Saxon churl," I went on.

"When we serve a lord, we should follow his example, yes?" Brother Simon inquired.

Again, I agreed.

"So where do we find the example? God is the Lord we should all serve - kings, barons and knights - in return for all that we receive, but as Christians we believe it's our Lord Jesus who shows us the example of how God behaves. Do you know that once, when the Lord Jesus was at table with his followers, like a baron in his hall with all his knights, he got up, stripped to his tunic, took a bowl of water and a towel and washed the feet of everyone there?

"That's what we're remembering when the Abbot washes our feet here in the monastery each week. If the Lord of all creation can wash feet, then no noble on earth should be too grand to dig the earth. Read the Bible, John! It says that if anyone wants to be great, they must be the servant of all."

* * *

But reading the Bible was not, unfortunately, coming easily. In fact it wasn't coming at all. I had been taking instruction from Brother Peter for weeks but I was still struggling with the simplest of Latin sentences. Eventually even the thought of my daily lesson made me feel sick. I think it must have been that feeling of sickness – a real churning in my stomach – that finally pushed me over the edge. It was a hot morning in the middle of July. The whole world seemed to be blazing with light and life, and I was imprisoned with a sweating, bad-tempered monk squinting at strange words in the gloom.

"I hate this!" I said suddenly. "I'm not doing it any more! Why do I have to do this? I'm not going to be a monk. It's stupid. I hate this place. I hate these lessons."

I glared at Brother Peter's round face, wondering what I'd ever seen in it that had made me feel welcome in the monastery. I wasn't frightened of him, although he was such a big, powerful man, but I was wary of what might happen next. I tried to read his expression. There was certainly anger gathering there, and his tanned face seemed to get even darker as if all his blood were pumping into it. Then he shouted too, but what he said astonished me.

"Do you think I don't hate it too? Do you think I want to be here, trying to teach a boy who doesn't want to learn? Do you think there aren't other things I'd rather be doing?"

He glowered at me as if the situation were all my fault.

"Like what?" I asked.

He swished his habit angrily for a while, then stopped and looked at me strangely, as if weighing up a possibility.

"Come with me, John," he said at last.

A few minutes later we were in the cloister - the quadrangle at the heart of the monastery. Although not even proper novices were supposed to spend time there, I had a strange position at St Mary's. No one was quite sure what I was, and Brother Peter's confidence in leading me round the covered walk that surrounded the open square must have forestalled any criticism. Several monks were studying in the north side of the walk but few of them looked up, and those that did quickly went back to their reading. Brother Peter took me to a cupboard in the wall. It was full of huge books. He heaved one down and led me away.

We went to a small room off the cloister that had nothing in it but a high writing desk. My father had one at our Hall that the clerk used if there were any documents that needed writing.

"This is a Scriptorium," Brother Peter told me, indicating the room. "Dare I ask you what the Latin word scribo means?"

"'I write'," I answered.

"Quite so, boy. This is the room in which I write. The word can also mean 'I draw'. Sometimes I draw here. And sometimes I paint. Look."

He placed the heavy book on the sloping surface of the desk, and I stood at his elbow as he opened it.

I gasped. The page was covered in carefully formed Latin writing, but at least a quarter of it was glowing with colour.

"It's beautiful!" I whispered.

It was a picture of monks working in the fields, harvesting corn with sickles, but there was so much detail that I couldn't take my eyes off it. There were tiny creatures poking their noses out between the stalks; there were delicate shapes of birds riding the air; even the expressions on the monks' faces were precise. I thought I recognised one.

"Is that Brother Thomas?" I asked.

Brother Peter smiled and nodded.

The colours were dazzling - rich red and blue and green - and there was even real gold gleaming from the page.

"Did you really do this?" I asked at last.

"Yes," he said. "I finished it early last year."

"The picture?"

"The book!"

I spanned the thickness of the volume with my hand.

"All of it?"

"All of it!"

"How long did it take you?"

"Nearly two years."

"Is it a Bible?"

"Yes. Can you read any of it, John? This is a great letter 'D'."

He drew his finger lightly over a shape that seemed to frame the painting. I hadn't noticed it before, but now I realised it was the first letter of the first word on the page.

"Are there more pictures?" I asked.

He barked - the first laugh I'd heard from him in weeks - and carefully he began to turn the pages. There were so many pictures I lost count. Some were of everyday scenes around the monastery; some Brother Peter explained were illustrating the Bible stories; in one I even spotted Brother Peter's own face - one amongst many in a crowd.

"It's the people of Jerusalem welcoming our Lord Jesus. They're waving palm-tree branches," he explained.

"But you don't live in Jerusalem!" I said.

"When I was painting that picture, I did," he told me. He closed his eyes as if remembering it. "Or at least I felt as if I did. I could feel the sun on my face. I could hear the crowds laughing and shouting. I could even smell them - and they didn't smell too good, I can tell you."

We both laughed.

"Imagination's a wonderful thing, John," he said. "It can take you anywhere."

We spent the whole of our study time searching for new pictures in the book. Sometimes Brother Peter would tell me the Bible story behind a picture, but mostly we just looked.

When he finally closed the book and said we would have to go, I asked, "Are all the Bibles like that?"

"The ones that I copy out."

"Don't other monks do it?"

"Not in this monastery. There are other monks here who copy the words, but I'm the only one who can paint. Or wants to, it seems. But in other monasteries it is done. It's called illumination. Have I taught you the Latin word lumen?"

"Yes," I said, surprised that I could remember. "It means 'light'."

"That's right, boy. And it can mean much else besides - a lamp to show the way, the brightness of daylight, glory, clarity, even life itself. For me, that's what illumination brings to the words on the page. That's why I do it. But lumen can also mean 'ornament'. I'm afraid that's all that some of the brothers can see in my pictures, and you'll have learned by now that we Cistercians do not approve of ornaments! For the other brothers copying the words is their work, their drudgery - they do it instead of digging or cleaning. For me, illumination is my study - my meditation on God's Word and his world."

As we left the Scriptorium, Brother Peter stopped and looked at me for a moment as he had earlier on in our study room, when he'd seemed to be making a decision.

"Can you draw?" he asked.

I told him that I had no idea.

* * *

Next day, Brother Peter was waiting for me in the shed as usual but he wasn't seated, and he put a hand up to stop me sitting either. He crept to the doorway and peeped out. There was no one passing, so he beckoned and we crept away like naughty boys up to no good. I noticed he was carrying a bundle.

Cistercians are clever with water. They can take a simple river and dig gentle-running channels from it to feed fish pools or powerful ones to drive their water mills. They also take a channel through their monasteries to flush away the waste from the toilets and the kitchens. The part downstream of the waste is not a good place to be; but upstream, where the channel first enters the monastery compound, it's a pleasant bubbling brook. This was where Brother Peter took me. The brook entered between banks nearly as high as a man, and there was sufficient space at the bottom for us to sit by the running water and enjoy the morning sunshine. We settled down there, securely out of sight, and Brother Peter undid his bundle.

It contained a number of scraps that I recognised as vellum - the material the books were written on. They were odd shapes and must have been left over when the writing sheets were cut from the skin of the sheep. There was also a small bottle of ink and a quill pen.

"Watch!" he said, and with a few strokes he drew a heron in a corner of one of the pieces of vellum. It was astonishing to see the slim feather pen being used so cleverly in such a huge, rough hand and I asked him to draw something else, but he shook his head.

"Your turn," he said, and handed me the pen and vellum.

I'd never tried to draw before, apart from scratching the earth with twigs, or once using the point of my father's knife on a flat stone - for which I was badly told off. But I felt excited as I took the waxy feather shaft between my fingers.

"What shall I draw?" I asked.

"What does the Latin word amo mean?" he asked.

"'I love'," I said, confused.

"Good. Then draw something you love."

After a few minutes I showed him the result of my efforts. It was our Hall, with its steep roof. There were two figures beside it. I told Brother Peter the smaller was Arlette, and the taller my father.

"Where's his horse?" he asked.

"I'll need to practise before I can try a horse," I said.

"Very true, boy. Now what does amas mean?"

"'You love'," I answered.

"Just so. Then I'd better draw something."

He took the materials, and quickly created a picture of St Mary's church with its tower.

"Now, what does amat mean, John? Be full and complete in your answer."

"It means 'he, she or it loves'," I answered smartly.

"Correct! So, now it's your turn again. Draw something that God loves – the greatest 'he, she or it' of them all!"

"She?" I asked.

"All love is to be found in God," he told me. "The warrior love of a father, the hand-clasping love of a brother, the tender love of a mother – and a love so far beyond all thought of 'he' and 'she' that I suppose all we can say is 'it'!"

I thought for a moment and then I drew a stream, and a tree, and a large field full of dots.

"What are the dots, boy?" he asked.

"People," I told him. "You're in there somewhere, and me and Father and Arlette, and King Stephen and the Empress Matilda."

Chapter Seven

Turning tides

That session by the brook marked a turning point. We no longer met for study as if we were rival monarchs squaring up for a fight. Instead we met as fellow enthusiasts for everything we could see and draw. I told Brother Peter about the wonderful tapestry that hung in my father's Hall, which had been the dream world of my childhood, and with his help I managed to draw some of its scenes. And we didn't creep about in secret for long either. Once it became clear that we'd stumbled on a way of working together, Brother Peter had a long talk with the Master of Novices. He was actually one of the most senior members of the monastery - only the Sub-prior, Prior and Abbot ranked above him - and he was able to give permission for us to take our materials out of the monastery compound into the fields and woods.

He wouldn't have done that just so that I could learn to draw, of course, but Brother Peter was able to tell him that we were using our drawing as a way of learning Latin too. And it was true. Somehow Brother Peter was able to slip the language in almost incidentally as we talked about the things we were seeing and drawing.

Then there were the psalms - they were the main part of the offices the monks sang in church, and it turned out that lots of them had things to say about the wonders of God's world. So as we looked and wondered and drew, Brother Peter would teach me bits of the psalms in Latin, what they meant, and how to sing them in the special chant of the monks.

To my amazement, I recognised more and more of the psalms during the offices, and when I heard and sang the words that I'd learned by the river, or in a leafy glade, I could close my eyes and imagine I was there. As Brother Peter said, the imagination is a wonderful thing. And now that I could join in and get my breathing to go in time to its rhythm, I started to find the chant was not the dull sound that I had first thought. Somehow it seemed to flow through the whole of my body like the pulse of life and I began to see how Brother Simon had been so upset to be banned from joining in. In fact, the whole rhythm of the day at the monastery began to seem like the steady pulse of life, now that I was able to find something to enjoy in every part of it.

* * *

August was coming to an end. The heat felt like a weight. The air seemed thick and somehow unhealthy. Brother Peter and I had been in the fringes of the forest beyond the sheep pasture, searching for woodland insects to draw. As we'd watched them, Brother Peter had made up stories about their adventures in Latin for me to translate, and I'd added ideas of my own. But now it was nearly time for the late morning office and Brother Peter was in a hurry, as he had to see the Prior before church. He left me to bundle up our things and follow at a slower pace, so I carefully wrapped the ink bottle, rolled our work, then stood up ready to go. And that was when I caught sight of a movement among the trees.

I stood absolutely still, eyes and ears alert as a rabbit ready to run. There was a faint rustle, and another hint of motion like the passing shadow of a bird.

"Who's there?" I called.

My experience with my father had left me continually wary of the forest, and I feared more men at arms. But the figure that stepped from the cover of a tree trunk not half a dozen paces away was much nearer my own size. His clothing showed him to be a peasant, but it was so ragged that it barely covered him. He was swaying, his face was blotchy and shining with sweat and his hair was plastered to his head as if he'd been in the river. I took all of this in before I realized that I knew him.

"Master John - help me," he croaked, in Saxon.

It was Siward, my father's servant boy.

We stared at each other for a moment, then he took a step towards me and I did something that shocked me almost the moment I'd done it. I turned and ran.

"Help me, please!"

I heard the words, so weak that they could hardly be called a shout, but still I kept running - down the pasture, towards the distant shelter of the monastery walls. To begin with, I had no idea why I was running. But then words started to drum in my mind in time to my pounding feet, "Saxon churl! Saxon churl!" over and over again.

Panting and sweating, I carried our things back to the hut that was still designated as our classroom. I took a moment to calm my breathing, then I joined the file into church. Dinner, thanksgiving, rest and another office followed before it was time for the work I'd been assigned for the afternoon. It was an easy task - weeding the herb garden beside the Infirmary - and I knelt low to the earth, searching for the roots of the weeds and lifting them with far more care than was necessary. I felt as if I needed to slow everything down to help me think. For the last three hours I'd been unable to get those words out of my head - "Saxon churl". Why had I said them? Why had I run? Neither had I been able to wipe Siward's sweating face from my mind.

I had only been working a little while when there was a commotion and I looked up to see two brothers striding towards the Infirmary door. One was grunting under the weight of Siward's body. I bent quickly to hide my face, but it was unnecessary. The boy's arms were swinging loosely, and his eyes were closed.

"Is he dead?" I asked, when the brothers came out again. My voice trembled. "No point in taking a corpse to the Infirmary, brother," one of them replied.

He explained that they'd been sent to tend the sheep and had found the lad collapsed at the edge of the pasture.

"Looks like fever. He's in a bad way."

"Did he say anything?" I asked.

"He's barely breathing – I doubt he'll ever speak again. God have mercy on him."

We all said "Amen" and the monks returned to their flock.

I weeded the same patch over and over, practically turning the dry earth into dust, and as I did I prayed: "Please make him better," and "Please forgive me." The explanation for my behaviour was finally forcing itself on me as I worked, and it was an explanation that made me feel sick at heart. I had grown up with Saxon children and, having no brothers or sisters, they'd been my only playmates. But I had always lorded it over them. I had played the lord and they had played the peasants as we acted out the adult world around us. I had bossed them unmercifully in all our games. If a hero were to be played, I would take the part without question. In any competition, I must win. And when I had had enough, the game was over. Saxons were servants and Normans were lords – so how could I now let Siward see me at St

Mary's labouring like a churl? Shame had sent me running from him.

I wrestled with a different shame through the rest of the afternoon. I barely ate supper and attended to nothing in the reading over our silent meal or in the singing of the two evening offices - Latin seemed an unknown language to me again. And when we rose for the first office of a new day, I had not slept at all. By the time the morning Chapter meeting was over and the sky was turning grey in expectation of the dawn I knew what I must do, and I asked to speak with Father Jerome.

He took me to a little room next to the Chapter House called the Parlour - the only place in the monastery set aside for conversation.

"Father Jerome," I began at once, "I think a boy was brought to the monastery yesterday with a fever. I was working in the Infirmary garden when he arrived."

"Ah yes, a bad case," the Novice Master replied, sadly. "Camp fever. Brother Peter has seen him, and that is what he thinks it is. He knows something of these things and has given advice to the Infirmarer."

"Camp fever?"

"I fear it often breaks out among bands of soldiers."

"But the boy can't be a soldier, surely," I said.

"Who can tell what his story is, dear brother? He hasn't opened his eyes as yet."

The thought that Siward might have some awful disease made what I intended to say all the more difficult, and I was tempted to pretend I had only wanted a report on his health.

"Well, Brother John?" the Novice Master prompted.

I stared at him for a moment, then I committed myself.

"Father, may I go to the Infirmary and nurse the boy?" I asked.

His long face tilted slightly to one side and his normally cheerful expression became grave.

"I must consult the Abbot," he said, after a pause. "Go to your work, John, and I will speak to you later in the morning."

It was after the next office that Father Jerome called me to the Parlour again.

"The Abbot has decided that it would be unwise for you to attend the invalid," he announced.

My head told me I should be relieved, but that was not how I felt.

"I don't understand," I said. "I thought it was good to look after the sick. It says in the Bible that looking after the sick is like looking after our Lord Jesus."

"Indeed it is, my brother," he replied, "but you must remember your situation here - our situation in having you."

"What do you mean?"

"Your father left you here to be protected from harm. The boy may well die, but more than that - so may those who attend him. We would not be fulfilling our duty to Sir Henry if we allowed you to take the risk."

"But Father—"

"No 'buts', John. The Abbot must be obeyed."

* * *

My study time with Brother Peter that day was almost as uncomfortable as our earliest meetings. I was moody and barely replied to Brother Peter's comments and questions. We had settled by the fish pond and for a long time I stared at my reflection in the mirror of its surface. Brother Peter asked me what was wrong, but I couldn't bring myself to share my troubles. At last he gave up and thrust a sheet of vellum and a quill into my hands.

"Here - take these and draw," he said. "I'll come back in an hour."

When he returned I had covered the sheet with attempts to draw a head.

"Those are good," he told me.

He was about to give them back, but then he suddenly peered at them more closely.

"They look like the boy with the fever," he said. "Do you know him?"

I took the pictures back and stared at them for a few moments. Then, choosing the best image, I picked up the quill and sketched a crown of thorns across its brow.

"Why did you do that?" Brother Peter asked, quietly.

I held on a moment longer, then told him everything – what I'd done, what I'd thought, what I'd tried to do earlier that morning, and what the Abbot had said. Brother Peter sat beside me and closed his eyes. He stayed like that for a while, then he told me to wait by the pool and he would speak to the Abbot.

Half an hour later, I was walking between the Infirmary beds with a bowl of water and a cloth over my arm. There was only one patient – the others had been sent back to their normal dormitory for safety. I knelt at Siward's side and bathed his face. He stirred slightly and muttered, but he didn't open his eyes. The Infirmarer had told me that the boy had not regained consciousness since the previous day.

"Siward," I'd said. "He's not 'the boy' – he's called Siward."

All that day and the next I sat by Siward's bed, bathing him from time to time, following the Infirmarer's instructions, trickling water between his dry lips.

It was on the second night, after the candle was lit and the last office had been said, that Siward suddenly opened his eyes. I said his name and he looked at me, slowly focusing on my face.

"Master John," he gasped.

I helped him sit up a little and gave him some water to drink.

"Thank you, master, that's kind," he said, and now that he'd drunk something to ease his throat his voice was almost normal.

The village Saxon sounded comforting and homely, and it felt good to reply in the same language.

"I'm sorry, Siward," I said, softly. "I'm sorry I ran away."

"No, Master John," he replied, wrinkling his brow. "You mustn't worry about that."

"*Brother* John," I told him. "You must call me brother. We're all brothers here."

He looked puzzled and unsure, and we were quiet for a few moments. Then I asked what had happened to him. His eyes filled with tears as he told me how a war band had raided our village and rounded up everyone who hadn't managed to flee. They'd been threatened with torture until they'd revealed where anything of value was hidden. Even then, most had been killed. Everything had been stolen and the whole place burned to the ground, even my father's Hall. Siward had only been saved because one of the warriors had wanted him for a slave. He'd been dragged behind the man's horse with a rope around his neck. But soon after, the men in the band had begun to fall ill. They'd been forced to camp in the forest and one by one they'd started to die. Eventually the ones who were left were so weak he'd been able to escape. But not long after, the sickness had taken him too. He'd been wandering aimlessly in the forest with no idea where he was when he'd found me among the trees.

Relief that Siward had revived and that I was safe at St Mary's seemed small comfort compared with the sorrow of knowing that my home was now nothing but charred wood and blackened stone. I hadn't missed our village for a long time, I realised, but now I knew it was gone all my longing for it rushed back. I closed my eyes and pictured the beautiful tapestry with all its creatures being eaten by the flames. And I thanked God that Arlette had been safe in the castle when the raiders came.

"Have you had word from Sir Henry?" Siward enquired, softly.

I opened my eyes and told him that I had not.

"And your father, Siward?" I asked. "Have you heard anything?"

"He can't write, nor I read," he replied. "There's no way of knowing."

"Do you miss your father, Siward?" I asked.

His eyes filled with tears again.

"And the rest of my family," he said.

"I miss my father too," I murmured.

We were quiet for a while, and Siward's eyelids began to droop.

"Brother John," he whispered, "I'm feeling tired now."

As he went to sleep I took his hand, and slowly I began to sag and nod in my seat.

Cramp and clear August sunlight woke me early the next morning. The hand that I still held was stiff and cold. I loosed my grip and it stayed where it was, rigidly moulded – a dead object. I got up to call for help and saw the Infirmarer muttering and writhing on a bed further down the room. I began to walk towards him but as I did the floor seemed to lurch sideways, my head spun and I sensed myself plummeting downwards.

When I woke, I was lying on one of the Infirmary beds, and Brother Peter was bathing my forehead. He told me I had been in the grip of the fever for a week. The Infirmarer had died, and so had the brother who'd carried Siward down from the pasture.

"It seems to have stopped there, God be praised," he said. "There have been no new symptoms. All the victims' bedding and clothes have been burned. The Abbot ordered that the Infirmary be closed to everyone but me, and I have stayed with you all week."

I struggled to sit and drink.

"Why didn't you die?" I asked.

"Why didn't you?" was his reply.

My head was pounding, but memory started to return and I recalled how Siward had seemed to recover, had sat up, talked and drunk as I was doing now and still had died. I took a deep breath and felt far from sure that I was out of danger.

"I prayed so hard," I said. "All the time I sat with Siward I prayed that he'd be healed."

Brother Peter took my hand as I had taken Siward's in mine, and I felt his powerful grip.

"There are many kinds of healing," he said. "Perhaps there was a healing granted here."

* * *

I didn't die, but summer did. As I grew stronger the fierceness of the sun weakened, and the air freshened. The harvest was in, fields were cleared, wood gathered, and outdoor activity at St Mary's became rarer. So did my wanderings with Brother Peter, although I was soon fit enough to resume them. But as autumn progressed we found another activity. My teacher thought that I had advanced sufficiently in my artistic skills to begin to paint. So we moved our lessons from the outdoors to the Scriptorium and I was allowed to try my hand at adding colour to my efforts. Brother Peter allowed me to watch him at work on the next Bible he was copying and illuminating. And because he was teaching me, we were allowed to talk.

I watched, hardly daring to breathe as his right hand moved confidently over the page, the curved scribe's knife in his left hand holding the wavy vellum straight as he worked on it. He could dip his quill pen into the horns of red and black ink that hung at the side of his chair without even looking. When he had finished a passage, he would read it to me, and I would follow it in the Bible he was copying from to check that he had made no mistakes. Then he would ask me if there was anything I didn't understand - in the Latin or the story. Sometimes, when it was time to put in a picture, we would discuss what it should be. And once he even did a picture of me giving some bread and fish to our Lord Jesus to feed the crowds.

Then winter came, and with it the first word from my father. Because it had to do with the war I read the letter to Brother Peter, knowing his interest. To me, the most important news was that my father was well and had escaped uninjured from a battle at Winchester in September, but I couldn't help thinking that Brother Peter paid more attention to another outcome of that battle. My father wrote that the Lady of the English had been defeated by the forces loyal to King Stephen and as she had been retreating, her half-brother, Earl Robert of Gloucester, had been captured. This had produced a kind of stalemate. Matilda still had King Stephen in prison, but Stephen's supporters now had Matilda's most powerful supporter under lock and key. Just before Father had sent his letter, at the beginning of November, Matilda had made a deal to release King Stephen in exchange for her half-brother. So as the year of Our Lord 1141 came to a close it seemed that Matilda's brief time as ruler of England, too, was over. But to the civil war, with all the death and suffering it caused, and to the absence of my father, there seemed no end in sight.

Chapter Eight

A clink of coins

A whole year passed – a year in which I heard only a handful of times from my father. Reading the big, clumsy writing in his letters I learned that after Matilda's rout at Winchester he had seen little real fighting. The civil war was being played out in a series of sieges and counter sieges with armies marching from one to another, eating the stores of every community on the way. As my father had predicted, it was the ordinary people who were suffering, not knights like him. When there was fighting, it was only the peasants who died in any great numbers. And in the villages they'd left behind it was the peasants' families who starved. For far too long there had been too few men to sow and harvest the crops and now the effects were beginning to tell. Food was desperately short in many areas and always under threat from passing war bands – either the armies of the royal rivals, or gangs of marauders just out for what they could get.

Siward's story wasn't the only tale of murder, robbery and destruction. It was repeated far and wide, and it wasn't easy to tell who the culprits were. Some were foreign mercenaries, mostly Dutch, mostly brought in by

King Stephen to fight in his armies. They cared nothing for Saxons, Normans, or anything in this island apart from its wealth. All they were interested in was their pay and whatever they could make on the side. Of course, my father didn't write these awful tales in his letters. Brother Peter and I learned them from the travellers who called at the monastery from time to time - merchants coming to buy our produce of wool or corn, or the labourers and craftspeople who came to help with the continuing building work.

The whole point of St Mary's being 'in the wilds' was that it was cut off from the outside world, so the monks were not supposed to have anything to do with visitors unless it was absolutely necessary. But Brother Peter had a way of not quite following Cistercian rules. The agreement he'd come to with Father Jerome about my study arrangements was typical. It didn't dawn on me for quite some time that not only was the arrangement good for me and my education - it also gave Brother Peter freedom. Over the months, the other brothers became used to seeing us together in unusual places, doing unusual things and so they stopped wondering what we might be up to. Brother Peter also had a natural air of authority - I'd seen it on the day Father and I had arrived - and that tended to stop people asking questions. So when there was a visitor to the monastery who might have some news, Brother Peter would usually find some way of passing a few words.

One dull and rainy day, however, early in the year of Our Lord Jesus 1143, I spied a merchant whom Brother Peter would not be able to question. I knew this because I'd just seen my teacher leading a working party down the valley with axes over their shoulders, obviously on their way to fell some timber. They wouldn't be back for well over an hour. I was in a good position to see the merchant approaching as I'd been sent to clear some winter debris from the channel that brought water into the monastery site to flush the drains. The blockage was outside the furthest boundary wall – the one that barred the main track into the site. I was working there, within sight of the track, when the merchant led his small train of pack mules up to the Gatehouse and was let in. I was on my own. No one would know if I spoke to the merchant, and I thought my friend Brother Peter would be pleased if I could give him some news from the world. It would be like giving him a gift. So I decided that if the merchant came out again before the monastery bell rang to call us in from our work, I would exchange a few words with him.

The rhythm of the monastery day had given me a good sense of time in the 20 months I'd now been there, and I judged that our work period was nearly over. I was resigning myself to not having any gift to give my friend, when I heard the grind and creak of the monastery gate and saw the merchant emerging, followed by his mules roped together in a line and with their packs full to bursting. In such a time of need, St Mary's was one place where corn could still be found. Our army of harvesters had not been marched away and our granaries were full. I stood up to meet the man, but then I noticed the monastery Porter, pausing to look at me for a moment. It occurred to me that there might be prying eyes elsewhere, and without Brother Peter at my side for protection I didn't want to risk a scolding. So I waited until the gate was closed and the merchant had forded the river – quite a tricky business with the mules and the river in full winter flow. The track curved out of sight behind a bluff, just on the far side of the river, and I decided to catch up with him there so that we could talk unobserved.

I let him get round the bend and then followed. I hauled my habit up to avoid the water and placed my feet carefully on the large stone blocks that formed stepping stones across the icy river. My feet were already soaked and numb from working at the channel and I was afraid that they would be so clumsy with cold that I might slip and fall. I moved slowly, and thought the merchant might now be too far ahead for me to catch him. But when I rounded the bluff, I stopped dead. Only a hundred paces ahead the mules were standing still in the middle of the track, their breath rising like smoke. The merchant was sitting on a rock with his back to me. There were many rocks and bushes beside the track and the scene was so strange and unexpected that I instinctively ducked out of sight.

I didn't know what to do next, but as I peeped from my hiding place to assess the situation I saw someone else step from cover a little further up the track, beyond the merchant. He was wearing a monk's habit and he walked down the track towards the merchant holding out a large, heavy looking bag. The merchant stood and as he took the bag I heard a clink like coins. The monk's hood was up, so I couldn't see who it was, but then he spoke and his words carried clearly through the frosty air.

"Hand it over at Far Grange, as usual. You'll get your commission. We'll have more on your next visit."

The voice was unmistakeably that of Brother Hubert, a novice no longer but now a full monk.

I had heard that voice frequently since he and Brother Simon had had their fight. It was cold and commanding, but unlike Brother Peter it didn't have a natural authority. If people jumped to obey when Brother Hubert spoke, I felt it was from fear of retribution if they didn't. The more I'd seen of Brother Hubert and his ways, the more impressed I'd been that Brother Simon had stood up to him that day in the fields. I'd also been impressed that Brother Simon had not risen to the bait again, despite the whispered insults to Matilda that I'd often heard Brother Hubert hiss in my friend's direction. There seemed more nobility in ignoring them than in disturbing the peace of St Mary's with another clash.

The merchant gave a slight bow and led his mules on up the track. Brother Hubert watched him for a moment, then the bell from the monastery rang and he turned towards the river. He passed within feet of me, but I was well hidden and he clearly suspected nothing. I gave him a head start then hurried to collect my tools and re-enter the monastery. As I passed through the gateway, a monk came hurrying down a flight of steps and bumped me.

"Make way, fool!" he snapped.

It was Brother Hubert. I stepped aside and he was about to go on, when he turned and looked at me closely.

"Where have you come from?" he demanded.

His eyes gripped mine, and I felt sweat rising all over my body as I told him about the blocked channel.

"Have you been anywhere else?"

"No - nowhere," I answered him.

I had my hood up to keep me warm, and I was glad that it shaded my reddening face. He stared at me a moment longer, then marched away. I took a deep breath to steady myself and looked round to see where he'd come from. The steps led up to the room that was built over the arch of the Gatehouse.

* * *

A couple of weeks later I was working with Brother Simon, also a full member of the monastery now, because he was teaching me a new skill. We were in the forge - a wonderful place to be in the winter because of the heat. It was the forge that used up much of the firewood the brothers cut from the forest. In the monastery itself, simple living meant putting up with the cold. On this day our task was repairing and replacing tools ready for the coming year. Brother Simon and a lay brother who was a skilled blacksmith were teaching me some of the basics. Unfortunately, there was another monk with us - Brother Hubert. I was glad of the lay brother's presence, as there was a strained atmosphere between the other two that felt hazardous in a place offering so many possibilities for injury. Brother Hubert had already swung very close to my friend, holding a red-hot length of iron in a pair of tongs.

"Have a care, brother!" the blacksmith had called out, seeing the danger.

"People who get in the way only have themselves to blame," was all Brother Hubert had to say. But he said it glaring at me.

Thankfully, a few minutes later a novice stepped into the forge and called to Brother Hubert above the noise of the bellows.

"Father Prior has need of you, Brother," he shouted. "You are to go to the Gatehouse."

Brother Hubert dropped what he was doing with a clatter and gave me a nasty look.

"Finish that, boy," he said.

When Brother Peter called me 'boy', it felt warm and loving, but on Brother Hubert's lips it made me sound like a slave. I went to pick up the sickle he'd been working on but Brother Simon put a hand on my arm.

"Leave it," he said. "I'll see to it."

As he worked away at the grindstone, sharpening the sickle blade, I asked him what went on in the Gatehouse.

"It's where Father Prior does his business with the outside world," he shouted above the noise of his grinding.

I considered this for a few moments. It seemed strange that the Prior, the second in command of the whole monastery, should call for such a newly professed monk to assist him. And I hadn't forgotten that Brother Hubert had bumped into me running down the steps from the Gatehouse after that strange transaction on the track.

"Has the Prior asked for Brother Hubert's help before?" I asked.

Brother Simon laughed.

"Often," he said. "It's usually when there's some merchant visiting. He's in charge of paying the masons who work here too."

"Why him? He's hardly a senior monk."

"Good question," Brother Simon answered. "Father Prior used to use him even when he was a novice. Perhaps it's because they're both from Boulogne. They seem to know each other from before they met here. Maybe there's a family link. Of course, such things shouldn't matter at St Mary's."

"All brothers in God's family."

"Quite - but some people still seem to value their earthly family above being part of a heavenly one. They say the Archbishop of York only got his place because he's King Stephen's nephew."

There was quite a walk from the forge back to the church for the next office and that gave me the opportunity to speak to Brother Simon away from the noise and clatter of our morning's work. I hadn't told anyone about my encounter with Brother Hubert on the track, but it had been troubling me and I needed to share it - especially since Brother Hubert's sharp words about 'getting in the way'. I couldn't help thinking that he had been reminding me of our collision at the foot of the Gatehouse steps, and that he was warning me about something more than being clumsy. It seemed to be the right time to share the story, and Brother Simon the right person to share it with. So after we'd walked for a few moments in the silence we were supposed to keep all the way back to church, I tugged his sleeve and began to explain. I was tentative at first, testing him out, but I could tell by his little words of encouragement that he was taking me seriously and soon I had told him everything.

We were joining the rest of the brothers by the time I finished, so Brother Simon wasn't able to reply, and as he pulled his hood further over his head it was impossible to see his face to gauge his reaction. He made no attempt to find me during the rest of the day, and I began to wonder if he was offended that I had been spying. I knew that he had reason enough to dislike Brother Hubert, but I also knew the Christian way was to put brotherhood in God's family above such disagreements. I started to convince myself that I had lost a friend by speaking out and so I found it hard to go to sleep that night, tired though I was. Eventually a gentle mixture of grunts, snuffles and snores told me that the novices were asleep, but I was still wide awake when a figure emerged silently from the shadows of the Novice House doorway and crept towards our mattresses. He came to my side, pulled back his hood and looked straight into my eyes. There was a full, sharp, winter moon and both our faces were clearly visible. He made a beckoning motion with his head and returned to the door. The intruder was Brother Simon.

"Where are we going?" I whispered, when we were outside in the cold night air.

"I've been thinking about what you told me," he replied. "I couldn't concentrate all the way through the afternoon offices, trying to work out what it might mean. Why would Brother Hubert have given the money in secret, outside the abbey? What did he mean about 'commission'? That seems to show that the merchant was doing a job for Brother Hubert, but what? Obviously something to do with handing the money bag over to someone else, but who, and why? And he said 'we'll have more' - there must be someone else involved. It all seems to point to an operation smuggling money out of the monastery."

"But where would Brother Hubert get it from?" I asked.

"That's what we're going to find out. We're going to the document room to look for clues."

"Do you think he stole the money from Father Prior when he went to help him? Surely the Prior would notice it was missing."

"Good point," Brother Simon replied. "If he's stolen from the abbey coffers, the only way he could get away with it would be to make a false record in the accounts book, and writing up the accounts book is exactly the job he goes to Father Prior to help with. You told me he said 'as usual' when he gave the bag to the merchant, and he regularly helps at the Gatehouse – he could have been slipping money out of St Mary's for months."

A monastery is not the kind of place where every door is bolted and barred. The brothers trust that God will watch over his people, and anyway the community has nothing that would be worth stealing apart from its stores of produce and the money made from selling them – and Brother Peter's beautiful books, of course. But who would steal from God? And who knew that the brothers were even here, in their distant valley in the wilds? Brother Simon and I found it easy enough to get into the document room and after a few minutes searching amongst the scrolls and volumes in its cupboards, my companion discovered what he was looking for. He opened a great leather-bound book and took it to the window where the moon lit up its pages as clearly as any lamp.

"What are you hoping to find?" I asked after several moments' silence.

"I don't really know," he replied, leafing through the book.

I caught sight of dates and saw the year before I'd arrived. The figures and entries meant nothing to me and all I could think was that those dates had been written in the book when I had been playing at home in our Hall, or singing with Arlette and practising my letters, or walking amongst the fields at my father's side, happily unaware of the existence of St Mary in the Wilds or of Stephen and Matilda and their war.

"Look!" said Brother Simon.

I focused my attention at the figures he was pointing out.

"See how much is being charged for grain - and here for wool? Now look at this." He leafed forward to the latest entry. "What do you notice?"

"It's less," I said.

"Exactly! Now look at the writing."

The monks were all taught to write in the same way, and the script was very similar, but it was possible to notice some differences. Some special little twists and flourishes appeared in the pages with the higher prices, but weren't in the more recent pages that all had lower prices for the produce.

"This is Brother Hubert's writing," he said, pointing to the recent entries. "And this is before he started writing up the ledger..." indicating the entries showing higher income.

"I don't understand what it means," I said. "Maybe the price has just gone down."

"When corn's in short supply?" Brother Simon asked. "Unlikely! I'll tell you what I think it means - we're still charging the same amount as we always have, but

Brother Hubert is writing a lower amount in the ledger and putting the difference into his money bag. That way, when the ledger is added up to see how much is supposed to be in the treasury, it will work out right. Brother Hubert is taking money out of the treasury, but he's taking the same amount out of the books – so the only person who knows the money's gone is him."

"And us, now," I said, excitedly.

But Brother Simon didn't seem so enthusiastic. He looked thoughtful.

"I could be wrong, of course," he muttered. "As you said, the price could simply have gone down. Perhaps Father Prior doesn't want to take advantage of the scarcity. Maybe the people can't afford to pay as much as they used to."

He scanned the most recent page again.

"Have you got a good memory, John?" he asked.

I thought of all the things Brother Peter had managed to cram into my brain.

"I suppose so," I said.

"Well, look at this. It's the amount the masons have been paid – remember it."

"Why?" I asked.

"Because the other job Brother Hubert has managed to get for himself is paying the masons."

Chapter Nine

The dangers of painting

Next to the Novice House was a narrow passage out of the cloister, and as I was about to re-enter my quarters, I was sure I saw a hooded figure lurking in its shadows. I glanced quickly at Brother Simon to see if he had noticed, but my companion was looking straight ahead as he made for the stairs to his own dormitory. When I looked back at the passage, the figure was gone. I didn't dare call to Brother Simon, even in a whisper, and next day I began to wonder if I had imagined, or even dreamed, that menacing shape in the shadows.

And to begin with, I wondered if I was imagining that Brother Hubert was keeping a special watch over us in the following days. But the occurrences soon became too much to be a coincidence – his eyes glared whenever either of us was near. For modesty's sake, and to avoid distractions, the brothers rarely looked into each other's faces and worked mostly with heads slightly bowed. There was no mistaking the unusualness of Brother Hubert's challenging stare. He made no attempt to hide the fact that he was watching, and it seemed that he wanted us to know as much.

I purposely didn't seek out an opportunity to work next to Brother Simon, in case it should arouse Brother Hubert's suspicions still further, but about a week after our night-time investigation, the Novice Master sent me to help Brother Simon stack some firewood for the kitchen. As I approached my friend, sure enough Brother Hubert appeared. He pushed back his hood to reveal his face, and gave me a long stare.

"Have you noticed how he watches us?" I whispered.

"Yes, he must know we're on to him."

There was no need to say who we were talking about. I told Brother Simon that I thought he may have seen us when we came back from the document room.

"He must be up to something," I said.

"I'd still like more proof. He could be watching us because he thinks we're up to something, after all."

"What are we going to do?" I asked.

Brother Simon led me past the kitchen and round the end of the lay brothers' quarters, out of sight of Brother Hubert.

"Do you remember how much the ledger said the masons are paid?" he asked.

I told him the amount.

"Good," he said. "Come with me."

He took me to the place where the masons were rebuilding the west end of the church.

The master mason seemed surprised when we approached, and rather annoyed to be broken off from his task. He was a short, broad-chested man who looked as if he could hurl the blocks of stone that his gang were busy trimming. He straightened his back and spat stone dust on the grass in front of us.

"Yes, brothers," he said, testily.

For a moment this surly response reminded me of something I'd forgotten over the long months - that Simon was a nobleman from the Countship of Anjou. Yet he was being spoken to by a stonemason as if he were no more than a Saxon farm hand. But if the situation seemed strange to me, Brother Simon didn't seem in the least put out.

"Excuse us," he said, meekly. "There's been a muddle with payments and Father Prior has sent us to ask if you have received your full money this month."

He confirmed that they had, and named a sum that was rather lower than the amount I remembered from the ledgers.

"Can I get on now," he said, and turned his back without waiting for an answer.

We turned away too, to find Brother Hubert striding towards us. He met us half way between the masons and the corner of the lay brothers' wing. He was holding up one of the little whetstones we use for sharpening our tools. We all carry them, in pouches hanging from our belts.

"I found this," he said. "I thought it might belong to one of you."

He was glowering accusingly at us, but Brother Simon wasn't to be cowed.

"I think you'll find it's your own," he said, pointing to the empty pouch at Brother Hubert's belt.

"How foolish of me," he said, with a sneer.

Clearly unashamed at having made up such an obvious excuse for following us, he put the stone in his pouch but showed no sign of leaving. He couldn't help himself glancing quickly over our shoulders at the masons, and I knew that if he went to talk to them the game would be up.

"Thank you, Brother," my companion said. "I'm sure you shouldn't waste any more time here now."

Brother Simon folded his arms and remained, unmoving in Brother Hubert's path. For the first time, I heard the imperious tones of the nobleman in my friend's voice, and I wondered if the two of them were going to take up their fight again. But perhaps Brother Hubert realised that he could be in enough trouble already without resorting to violence in the presence of a gang of masons for witnesses. Whatever the reason, he turned sharply and retraced his steps.

Brother Simon waited until he had disappeared round the end of the wall before he made his move.

"I think we all know where we stand now," he said. "Hubert is paying those masons less than he's entering in the ledgers and we can be sure that the difference is going into his money bag and out of the monastery. He's clearly collecting wealth, which breaks his vow of poverty. And he's clearly stealing, which breaks the law of God. The trouble is, it must also be clear that we're on to him. We'll have to act quickly or heaven knows what he might do - a man who's broken the trust of the community in such a way might do anything. We must ask to see the Abbot at once."

We met the Abbot in the upper room over the Gatehouse, and I wondered how Brother Simon would present the case without giving away our trespasses. But to my amazement he simply told the truth - that I had followed the merchant up the road without permission, that we had been creeping about the monastery at night contrary to the rules, and even that he had lied to the masons to find out their pay.

The Abbot was a very round man, and it was difficult to read his features as they seemed so small and indistinct in the middle of his large moon of a face.

"My son," he said to Brother Simon, "you have been punished once, for fighting with Brother Hubert, but I can see that your misdeeds on this occasion are of a different nature and for a different reason. I shall therefore treat them as a first offence - as they are for you, young Brother John. Now I must simply ask you both whether you recognise that disobedience and dishonesty are offences - to this community and to God."

Brother Simon bowed his head and responded, "Yes, my lord." And I repeated the words.

"Good," the Abbot replied. "Offence must never be given lightly, and will never be taken lightly. So let that be an end of that. Now, to the heart of the matter - let us send for Father Prior."

Father Prior was summoned, to whom we had to repeat our story. The Prior confirmed that indeed he had engaged Brother Hubert, shortly after he had begun his novitiate, to act as his clerk. He explained that he had known the brother's family and knew that Hubert had been an excellent manager of his father's estates before entering the monastery. He had trusted the young man completely and had not thought to question the amounts being entered into the ledgers. The Abbot then dismissed Brother Simon and me to our duties, and cautioned us to say only that we had had private business with the Abbot, should we be asked to account for our absence.

"There will be time enough to elaborate when the community is summoned," he explained.

* * *

It was the following day when all the monks and novices were called together. Even I was required to attend this council, Father Jerome told me, since the Rule stated that God often showed what was the best course of action to the young. We gathered in the upper room over the Gatehouse, as this doubled as a court for the community, the Novice Master told me, as well as the place of business with the outside world.

"Like the Moot Hall in our village?" I asked.

"Yes, Brother John," he replied. "And the Abbot presides as our lord, as your father would preside over his court in the Moot Hall. Just as your father would pass judgement there, it is for the Abbot to pass judgement here, after he has heard the advice of the community. And just as your father must exercise justice under the authority of Baron Gilbert and according to the laws of England, so the Abbot passes judgement under the authority of God and according to the ways of his kingdom."

I had stood at my father's side many times in the Moot Hall, but as I sat with Father Jerome on the long bench around the walls of the upper room I noticed one major difference. In the Moot Hall there was noise, chatter and bustle, until my father rose to speak. Here all waited in silence and stillness. Even when the accused entered, led by Father Prior, there was not a stir; except from me.

'What?' I cried, and Father Jerome hastily put a hand on my arm to quieten me.

"I'm sorry, John," he said.

In the centre of the room next to Brother Hubert stood Brother Peter.

I looked across to where Brother Simon was sitting against the opposite wall. We caught each other's eyes, and he looked astonished. I was so shocked that I barely heard what was being said as Father Prior went through the evidence Brother Simon and I had presented. But then he started to explain how the Abbot and he had decided that since Brother Hubert had implied he was not working alone, they would have the dormitories searched whilst the brothers were at work. After such a betrayal of trust, no one in the monastery was above suspicion and all mattresses had been searched. Money had been found hidden in the hay of Brother Hubert's bedding, as expected, but also in the mattress of Brother Peter.

The two accused were invited to speak to the community and explain themselves.

Brother Hubert simply stared at the wall, over the heads of the brothers and said in a flat voice, "I have been betrayed. A promise has been broken."

"What promise, my son?" the Abbot asked.

"I have nothing more to say, my lord," he replied.

"Well, Brother Hubert, in the courts of the princes of this world you might expect compulsion by torture, but here we will not seek to break your silence if you are determined to maintain it. And the princes of the world would impose mutilation or death for the crimes of which you and Brother Peter are accused. However, this court is not subject to their laws but to the laws of the Lord of mercy. Still, you must expect the severest punishment that our Rule allows. And so must you, Brother Peter, unless you can persuade this council to advise me otherwise."

Brother Peter's weather-darkened face was totally lacking in its normal self-assurance. He looked confused, helpless as a child and, criminal or not, I felt a great urge to cross the room and stand at his side. I remembered the power of his arms as he had held my father fast and galloped away with him to safety, how he had taught me to pray and paint and hear God's praises in Latin, French, Saxon or the sweet song of the river. It seemed that he was going to be as silent as Brother Hubert, and I found myself willing him to speak, even praying in that simple way I'd learned from him, "Dear God, let him explain. Let there be a reason."

At last he stirred himself and looked around the room at the community of his brothers.

"Why would I do it?" he asked. "What motive could I possibly have for stealing from you – for stealing from God?"

As I heard these words, I realised that in my heart I had no problem in associating the simple motive of greed with Brother Hubert. But Brother Peter was so clearly a man of openness, sincerity and simplicity, that some other explanation was needed for his theft.

As if rising to the challenge, the Prior stood and held up something that he had been keeping hidden beside him on the bench. It was the illuminated Bible that Brother Peter and I had spent so long poring over when I'd first learned of his gift.

"Luxury!" the Prior announced, opening the pages and showing the brilliant pictures to the room. "Our beloved Cistercian Order is an Order of purity and simplicity, yet this brother thinks that the word of God is in need of paint and colour and gilding. And look at this!"

To my amazement, he now held up some examples of my drawing and painting - scraps of vellum that Brother Peter had continued to collect for me and on which I'd been producing ever more competent and elaborate work over the past year.

"Given the great privilege of educating this young boy and the freedom to roam where he will and do as he likes with him, this is what he does! He leads him into his own way of luxury - and of heresy!"

He pointed out the detail of some of my pictures, showing how they were based on Bible stories, but that I'd used my imagination to explore them and interpret them so that there was more in them than could be found in the book. I remembered drawing some of the images and how doing them had made the Bible come alive for me so that I'd begun to learn its stories. I felt that, thanks to Brother Peter, I now loved some of them even more than the old songs Arlette used to sing me of knights and their battles and lady loves. Yet here was the Prior telling everyone that it was wrong and that it made Brother Peter evil.

"Who knows what debauchery such a man might be capable of," the Prior concluded. "Who knows what perverted pleasures he might have been planning to spend his money on with the help of his 'agent'?"

There was a buzz in the room, and I realised two things. First, the Prior had suggested that Brother Peter was in fact the principal thief and was somehow using Brother Hubert. Second, the rest of the community seemed to be supporting the Prior's view of Brother Peter's character. In a rush, I remembered all the times Brother Peter had assumed a natural command and ordered the other brothers around and I remembered something I'd noticed but not thought much of at the time - the little looks of resentment, the grudging agreements. I saw in a moment how Brother Peter's freedom to wander where he pleased and to do what he wanted with his pupil might have appeared very different to the rest of the community than it had to me.

I had been overjoyed, but the looks I saw around the room and words I heard showed very clearly that many of the brothers had felt otherwise.

The Abbot called for order and the room fell into respectful silence. The Prior sat down again and the Abbot invited Brother Peter to respond to what had been said. I was thankful to see that his face was no longer uncertain. It was angry.

"Everything I have done has been in the service of God, and under the guidance of God," he said. "If you condemn these pictures, then condemn the psalms that we sing each day! What are psalms if they're not pictures of praise drawn in words? Show me the difference between the psalmist's words and these pictures of John's!"

I bowed my head, embarrassed to find myself suddenly at the centre of the discussion, but I could hear that Brother Peter's words had not helped his case. There were no murmurs of approval, and the few comments that were made spoke of pride and presumption. Nothing was said to suggest that the Abbot should do anything other than regard the two accused as guilty, and punish them as severely as he thought fit.

Chapter Ten

Kidnapped

The brothers filed out of the Gatehouse in silence. But I stayed rooted to the spot. I couldn't avoid the feeling that I'd betrayed my friend. It made no sense - you can't betray someone if you don't know they're involved in something - but the feeling still stayed with me. For the first time in well over a year, I just wanted to hide away and cry.

"Dear Brother John, this must be very distressing for you."

I looked up and saw the long face of Father Jerome.

"It's a great sadness to us all," he went on.

"Really?" I said. "I thought some people were delighted."

I felt immediately sorry for the rudeness in my voice - Father Jerome had not been among those who had seemed eager to accept Brother Peter's guilt. I had instinctively looked across the room at him as the accusations were being made, probably because I trusted his judgement and I didn't know what to think myself. I had seen nothing but puzzlement in his expression.

"Ah," the Novice Master said. "You remember when Brother Hubert and Brother Simon turned their farming implements into weapons of combat?"

I nodded.

"That is not the only example of our little community falling short of paradise. We are only human, Brother John, and you must try to forgive us our failings as we try to forgive each other."

I found that I could not picture the satisfied faces of some of the brothers when Brother Peter had been found guilty, and think forgiving thoughts. But then, if Brother Peter had been found with the money, perhaps they were right to be satisfied that he was to be punished. I was so busy with my thoughts that I didn't pay much attention to where Father Jerome was leading me. It was the hour for study and I should have been going to Brother Peter in the Scriptorium, but the Novice Master led me to the Parlour. When I entered, I found Brother Simon was sitting on the stone bench that ran round the room. Father Jerome patted my shoulder, gave Brother Simon a meaningful look and then left us. I sat beside my friend.

"Is he guilty?" I asked.

There could be no doubt which of the accused I was referring to.

"Our Rule tells us that we should not presume to question the Abbot's judgement," Brother Simon told me, not meeting my eyes.

"But is he guilty?" I persisted.

"It seems very odd. Whoever is involved with Brother Hubert, Brother Peter is probably the last person I would have suspected."

"You don't agree about the painting and the luxury?"

"Not at all," Brother Simon answered, without hesitation. "He may do things differently from the rest of us, but just being different doesn't make someone a criminal."

"So is he guilty?"

"He had the money, John," Brother Simon said, sadly. "I don't know why he had it, but it was in his mattress. I'm sure the Abbot made his judgement on that and nothing else."

"So you think he's guilty."

Again, Brother Simon's eyes left my face.

"The Abbot has made his judgement," he said. "He is our Father under God, and we have promised to be obedient."

* * *

"Well I haven't promised," I said to myself, as I repeated this exchange in my mind that night, lying on my cold mattress.

I couldn't sleep, and I had come to a decision. I got up quietly and crept to the monks' dormitory. In the Parlour Brother Simon had explained to me that the two guilty monks wouldn't work, eat or worship with the rest of the community until the Abbot said otherwise, but they would sleep with the others as there was nowhere else for them to go. I made out Brother Peter's powerful shape curled on his bed. I was going to shake his shoulder as I had so often shaken my father's when I was troubled in the night, but I could see by the flickering light of the night candles that Brother Peter was still awake. I put my fingers to my lips and beckoned him to follow.

We left the dormitory by the day stairs that led into the gloom of the cloister, and I drew him into the shelter of the Parlour.

"Did you do it?" I asked him bluntly. "Tell me the truth."

The anger that had risen in him after the Prior's accusation seemed still to be burning.

"Do you think I did?" he snapped back.

"You had the money. The Abbot said you're guilty."

"Do you think I did it?" he insisted.

We were whispering, but there was such force in his voice that it felt as if he had shouted at me.

"I don't know," I said. "That's why I had to talk to you."

He seemed beside himself, desperate and angry, but not really angry with me. I didn't feel unsafe.

"John," he said, "I have promised that I will own nothing. Even my body is not my own, but is for the community to command through the Abbot. The books I have illuminated are not mine but are for the glory of God and the use of my brothers. Why should I collect wealth? I already have treasure enough in being able to enjoy God's world and praise him for it. And I have taken a vow of poverty - why would I break my promise? Broken promises destroy the world."

"What do you mean?" I asked.

"Look at England," he said. "The great ones in the land broke their promises to have Matilda as their queen not once but twice, and now everyone breaks their promise to everyone else as easily as stepping over a stream. There is no loyalty or trust left. There's nothing but chaos and anarchy in a land of broken vows."

He spoke with such passion that I could no longer doubt him. But my relief began to be soured by another anxiety, stirred up by his words.

"Does everyone break their promises now?" I asked.

He looked at me strangely then, as if suddenly remembering with whom he was talking, and put both his heavy hands on my shoulders.

"I'm sorry, John," he said. "This trouble is mine, not yours. I was forgetting myself. Even in the worst of times there are still men and women of honour to be found. Your father is a true knight - he won't abandon you."

We were quiet for a while. It seemed that neither of us knew what to do next.

"What will happen to you?" I asked at last.

"We shall be beaten, that's certain," he said.

I was horrified.

"That's impossible," I said. "Beating's a punishment for peasants."

"Our Lord Jesus is the Prince of Heaven, but he was beaten, John, and worse."

"But you've done nothing wrong!"

"Neither had he."

In the gloom, I sensed Brother Peter sink onto the stone bench around the wall. Then I heard him sigh from the shadows.

"The beating isn't what troubles me most," he said, at last.

"How can there be anything worse than that?" I asked.

"For something as serious as this," he said, "the Abbot may well order us to leave the monastery."

"And that's worse than a beating?"

"This community is my life, John. It's all I want. Without this, I'm nothing."

From the moment I'd met him Brother Peter had radiated power, authority and confidence but now, almost invisible in the darkness, he seemed lost, and I made another decision.

"You're not guilty, Brother Peter," I said, "and I'm not going to let them throw you out of your home."

All this time we'd continued our conversation in urgent whispers, but now he gave one of his barking laughs. It surprised us both and I shushed him, quickly.

"What can you do about it, boy?" he asked.

I realised that he probably had no idea of my involvement and I quickly explained what I knew.

"There's no question about Hubert being guilty," I said. "But someone else is involved with him, and it's not you. Whoever it is must have put that money in your mattress to cover their tracks. If I can find out who it is, then perhaps the Abbot will believe you."

"How are you going to do that?" he asked.

"Hubert talked about some arrangement at Far Grange," I said. "I'll go there and see what I can find out."

I knew he'd try and stop me, so before he could think I dashed for the door. The passage out of the cloister was only a few paces away and in a moment I was through it and among the outer buildings. The monastery was a confusing place even in daylight and my first thought was to use this fact to get out of Brother Peter's sight. So I didn't try to escape the compound at first but darted among the looming walls and angles, keeping to the deepest shadows until I felt sure no one could be on my trail. After a while I stopped and listened. Nothing. I decided it was time to make my break, but I didn't head for any of the gates or doorways through the perimeter wall. Instead, I clambered straight over it. It wasn't designed to keep out attackers and presented no difficulties to an agile boy. I dropped onto the frosty grass on the far side and listened again. Still no sounds of pursuit. The woods were a dark rampart beyond the fields and I ran towards them as fast as I could.

* * *

As soon as I was in the shadow of the first trees I stopped and bent over with my hands on my knees, panting for breath. The cold air rasped my lungs and I felt slightly sick. I could hear nothing but my thumping heart. I certainly heard no footsteps to give me warning. So when a heavy hand landed on my shoulder I yelped out loud, jerked upright and swung wildly with my fist. But the bulky body behind the hand moved with surprising speed and I staggered as I swiped at thin air.

"Whoa, boy – it's only me!"

The voice was unmistakeable.

"How did you get here?" I asked.

Brother Peter let out a barking laugh, and looking at his round face in the moonlight he seemed to be very pleased with himself.

"Well, you told me where you were headed," he said, "so I wasn't going to waste my time chasing you all round the buildings. I thought I'd simply come up here and wait."

I laughed too.

"But how did you know I'd come just here? I could have made for cover anywhere in the woods."

"Ah," he said, "that's a skill."

"Are you going to take me back? I won't go," I said, stepping away from him quickly.

He smiled.

"Take you back? I'd have to catch you first," he replied, "and you're much too slippery for that."

"What then? Why did you come after me?"

"Let's walk," he said. "I'm getting cold."

He set off further into the trees and I followed.

"Where are we going?" I asked.

"Far Grange – you don't know the way, but I do. I couldn't leave you to wander around in these woods on your own, could I? You'd get lost and freeze to death! It's my Christian duty to come with you, since I can't stop you."

"You're not trying very hard," I said.

We were walking shoulder to shoulder now in the cramped spaces between the trees and he could have grabbed me any time he wanted.

"There's a pathway just ahead and to the right, if I'm not mistaken," he said, ignoring me. "Sometimes monks are sent to the Grange on business or to see that the lay brothers are working as they should. I've been a few times. There are storage barns there. We can hide in one and see what we can find out."

I still had a fear of the woods and was very relieved to have his company, especially at night, but I made myself tell him he could go back to the monastery once he'd got me to the path.

"I don't want to get you into any more trouble," I told him.

"I couldn't leave a boy travelling alone at night," he said. "I'd be worried about you."

"As a Christian?"

"As a friend," he said.

A few moments later we reached the path.

"Come on," he said, "step out briskly or we'll freeze."

I didn't doubt what he'd said about his concern for me, and that it wasn't just about duty, but he did seem unusually eager.

"You're enjoying this, aren't you?" I said.

"Mm," he replied, "I suppose I am!"

We marched on in silence, our breath coming in big steamy clouds, and sweat starting to form beneath the thick material of our habits. I began to think about how he'd said that finding the right place to intercept me was a skill, about his strength and agility, about his commanding presence in the monastery, and about his almost hungry interest in the doings of the world.

"Have you always been a monk?" I asked.

"No," he answered.

I waited, but he offered nothing further.

"What were you before?" I prompted him at last.

"Something else."

Again, he didn't elaborate.

"Something you're ashamed of?"

"No."

"Then why don't you tell me?"

He thought for a while.

"It's just another life, John," he said. "It doesn't seem as if it's about me."

"How old are you?" I asked.

He laughed loudly.

"Blessed if I know," he said. "Somewhere in my fifties I should think."

I was going to ask where he'd been born, but suddenly he put a hand on my shoulder.

"Stop," he hissed. "Listen."

But it was too late. Three men at arms stepped out into the path, and when we swung round we found another two behind us. On either side, too, helmeted men in mail armour came towards us with swords in their hands. Even if we had been armed, a boy and a monk would have stood no chance against such a war band.

"Come with us," their leader ordered.

Our hands were quickly tied behind our backs, and they dragged us away among the trees.

Chapter Eleven

The bodyguard

We hadn't been staggering through the forest for many minutes before we began to hear sounds ahead – low voices, occasional clanks of metal, the snort of a horse, a crackling that sounded like fire. Soon the smell of wood smoke came to us, and as the trees began to thin we could see the glow of firelight. Suddenly a deep voice growled out a challenge from the shadows, and the leader of our captors gave his name.

"Patrol with prisoners," he explained.

"Pass!" the deep voice replied.

We were jostled into a broad forest glade. I could see several bonfires dotted around it and a scattering of tents, one in the centre much larger than the rest, and as my eyes began to pick out the details of the scene I realised that there were large groups of men huddled on the ground around each fire. The patrol leader reported to a man who told him to leave us till the morning. So we were dragged towards the area where the horses were kept under guard at the edge of the glade. They knocked us to the ground, tied our feet together, then fastened longer ropes to our ankles and tied them to a nearby tree. The patrol leader fetched some cloaks and threw them over us, pulling our hoods over our heads for extra warmth.

"We don't want them dead in the morning," he explained when one of his men complained. "We want them to talk."

"Try to sleep," Brother Peter whispered, when they'd left us. "We'll see what the morning brings."

* * *

I couldn't see how I was going to sleep, lying on the frozen ground in such cold, but I must have done because I certainly woke up when I was kicked. I opened my eyes to see a harsh morning light filling the glade.

Someone shouted, "Get up!" and I was hauled to my feet.

I would have fallen over again if I hadn't been held tight, as I'd forgotten my legs were tied together.

"Stand still!" a man barked and knelt to unfasten my ankles.

I ached all over. Brother Peter was standing near to me, also being untied. The glade was full of activity. The fires had been stoked up and there was a smell of cooking. There was coughing and spitting, and the voices of men newly-woken could be heard cursing and calling to each other everywhere. Coloured pennants were flying from the tents, and some of their occupants were standing outside them giving orders, while servants carried food and flagons of ale into others. I could see neat piles of weaponry here and there and had been to Baron Gilbert's castle often enough to know that this was a military camp - men at arms gathered round the fires and knights in the tents. I had a sudden hope that maybe my father was somewhere here. I looked eagerly from tent to tent as we were led through the camp, expecting to see him any moment and be able to call out for rescue.

But by the time we reached the large tent in the centre of the glade I had seen neither him, nor any other of Baron Gilbert's knights. Outside the big tent was a collection of important-looking men, wrapped in fine warm cloaks. Their faces were like the faces of hawks - proud, sharp, without mercy or expression. I thought they must be the greatest of lords and I hardly dared look at them. They were talking to a seated figure, bowing slightly each time they spoke, and I knew that this person must be the greatest lord of all - perhaps it was even the King. All we could see of this figure was a richly-cloaked back and a large hood. It could have been a monk's habit if it hadn't been made of the deepest purple velvet, edged with ermine fur. As we arrived with our guards, one of the lords bowed to this mighty figure and whispered. The figure stood and turned towards us. My eyes caught a swirl of velvet; a flash of brilliant green brocade; a twinkle of pearls in the morning light; white, smooth, beardless cheeks; and a mass of violent copper hair.

"On your knees!" shouted one of the lords.

Our guards gave us no time to obey, throwing us down on earth frozen hard as stone. Our hands were still tied and my body hit the ground as if I'd fallen from a horse. I yelped.

"Silence!" the lord barked. "Silence before your sovereign!"

"Do homage to the Empress Matilda," another lord commanded, "the Lady of the English and your true monarch."

"Yes, yes, Robert," the Empress butted in – "that will do! I'm monarch of little more than a forest at the moment."

The voice was stunning. It was a woman's, without doubt, but there was such command in it that the lord was silent at once. And yet it wasn't shrill or harsh like a man's when he commands. There was such deep richness in it that I couldn't help looking up to see the face it belonged to. I glimpsed her green eyes, hard as a warrior's, before a foot pressed my face against the ground again.

"Explain yourselves!" demanded the lord she'd called Robert. "What were you doing in the forest? Who were you spying for? Who is your lord?"

"Brother, use your eyes," the Empress, cut in testily. "The man's a monk. His lord is the Lord of all creation. And this, by the looks of it is a monk's cub. They might say Mass for us, but I doubt they'll be any other use."

"My lady, they may be in disguise," her brother replied.

"Yes, my dear Earl, and you may someday be worth more than a buffet around the ears."

She took a step towards us.

"Come on, then, get up," she ordered. "Show us your faces and let's see if you have a monkish look about you."

With our hands still bound and after a night on the ground it was a struggle to move.

"Oh, come on, give them some help, you clods!" Matilda cried, and at once the guards pulled us to our feet. "Cut them loose," she ordered. "Are you frightened they're going to batter you with prayers?"

The guards started fumbling to untie our hands.

"Cut! I said, cut!" she shouted. "Oh come here - come here at once!"

She called us like dogs, and we came obediently. She drew a sparkling dagger from her belt.

"Turn round!"

We did so and I felt my wrist being taken in a strong grip as she cut through my bonds.

"If you want something doing, do it yourself," she muttered. "Now turn round again and let's see your faces. Take those hoods off, you look like a pair of ghouls."

We did as we were told and the Empress froze. She was staring at Brother Peter, seemingly oblivious to me or anyone else. Her hard green eyes softened and wrinkled at the corners, then the corners of her thin mouth began to twitch. A harsh little laugh burst out of her. She swallowed as if trying to control herself, but then another laugh came. Her eyes began to sparkle, and Brother Peter suddenly let out one of his braying donkey laughs. Then they were both laughing together. She lurched forward and put her hand on Brother Peter's shoulder to steady herself. Several of the lords made a move towards her but she waved them away with her other hand. Everyone stared in amazement.

When at last they'd exhausted themselves, the Empress took a step back, giving Brother Peter a powerful slap on the arm as she did so. She looked him up and down and her face was beaming.

"Well, thank God for a priest!" she said. "Is it really you, Peter? You're the best thing I've clapped eyes on since I set foot in this wretched country. What have you done to your hair, man?"

Brother Peter, too, was beaming. He tapped the shining skin of his tonsured scalp.

"Blown away by the wind of the Holy Spirit, my lady," he said.

"Nonsense - you're just going bald, old man. But I have to say joining a monastery's a pretty clever way of disguising it. Come on, let's have breakfast - I'm starved. You must be frozen. Bring them some decent clothes - this man should be dressed like a prince, not a beggar."

* * *

Brother Peter declined the fine clothes that were offered him and the meat, and out of loyalty I did the same. But we did gratefully allow ourselves to be wrapped in warm cloaks and made a hearty breakfast of bread and cheese in front of a crackling fire by Lady Matilda's tent. As we were eating, she seemed to take notice of me for the first time.

"How old are you, young monk cub?" she asked.

I told her I was 13.

"Almost a man," she said.

She took my face between her hands and looked at me as a knight might look at a horse. Then she squeezed my biceps with her strong fingers.

"And a fine man you'll make, I'm sure - especially if old baldy here has your training. I've got three boys, you know," she told me. "The eldest's nearly 10 now. I hope he turns out as fine a young man as you, monk cub. What's your name?"

"John, my lady."

"A good, honest name. My eldest's called Henry."

"That's my father's name!" I said.

"And mine," she told me.

"King Henry – the Lion of Justice," I replied.

"Ah, you know your history, monk cub John. I can guess who taught you that. So you know about my father – tell me about yours. Is he a farmer?"

"A knight, my lady," I told her proudly. "Sir Henry Fitzherbert. Our family came to England with the Conqueror – your grandfather."

"Fitzherbert?" she said, thoughtfully. "I can't think of any Sir Henry Fitzherbert who fights under my banner."

My head bowed in embarrassment.

"My father fights for King Stephen," I said quietly.

"*Count* Stephen, I think you mean," she corrected. "My cousin is merely the Count of Boulogne, monk cub. He is no more a king than you are."

"The boy's father has sworn to give service to Baron Gilbert," Brother Peter explained.

"And Baron Gilbert has sworn to give service to *me* although he finds it convenient to forget the fact – he and all the rest of them."

Her voice had become hard and commanding again and her chin jutted as if she dared anyone on earth to defy her. She was fearsome – the daughter and granddaughter of mighty warriors - and my face must have shown some alarm.

"Don't worry, John," she said. "I won't have your head cut off for the sake of your father - although I could, and don't you forget it. Your father is only doing what a true knight should - keeping his word. And if only the barons of England had followed his example, we wouldn't be in this mess."

She took hold of a piece of meat and gnawed at it like a wolf until there was nothing left but bone, then she threw the bone in the fire and drank off a goblet of wine as if it were water. I suddenly noticed that Brother Peter was looking at her with the strangest of expressions. It was something like the way he looked when he was completely engrossed in a painting.

"Poor Matilda," he said. "You deserve better than this."

"Don't 'poor Matilda' me, baldy!" she snapped, but she didn't look angry. "It should be 'poor England'. It's England that deserves better than all this cheating, and bad faith—"

She jumped up and twirled around with her arms outstretched and her fists clenched.

"It makes me so *angry*!" she cried. "What have they *done* to this country with their broken vows? There's so much evil here the people are saying Christ and his saints must be sleeping."

"Weeping, more like," Peter replied.

"Well, the people are weeping - that's for sure," the Empress told him. "They're weeping with starvation this winter."

We were interrupted by the man she'd called her brother. He marched up to us with a jingle of mail and accoutrements and bowed deeply.

"My lady, we must have our orders. The sun is well up and we have far to travel today."

"Yes, yes, Robert," she snapped. "Time enough - you nag worse than a nursemaid."

"How goes the war?" Brother Peter asked her.

For the first time, she looked less than certain of herself.

"Not well, my friend," she said.

"Your majesty!" Earl Robert protested. "You surely do not intend to discuss such matters with this, this—"

He broke off, lost for words to describe Brother Peter.

The Empress stood, and looked the Earl squarely in the eye. I realised, now, how tall she was - and every inch a monarch.

"Let me tell you," she said with quiet menace, "I would trust this man, for whom you can find no description, with my life - and the life of my children - which is more than I can say for you, or for anyone else in this camp."

The brother and sister glared at each other for a moment. He was much older than her, perhaps older than Brother Peter, but even a boy like me could tell she was the stronger character. Nonetheless, Earl Robert was not going to back away. After a moment she gave a snorting laugh and slapped his shoulder.

"Oh come, Robert, let me introduce you and set your heart at rest."

She gestured to Brother Peter, who got to his feet.

"Peter," this is my half-brother, "Robert, Earl of Gloucester, the dolt who got himself captured at Winchester."

"Your majesty!" cried the Earl.

"Oh yes, yes, I know - bravely commanding the rear guard to cover his sister's escape. Very dutiful, Robert. And you know I value you - after all I set Count Stephen free to get you back again. We made a mess of things at Winchester, that's for sure. I could have done with you then Peter."

"A monk!" Earl Robert scoffed. "We needed more than prayers that day, my lady."

Matilda laughed.

"Not always a monk, eh Peter?" she said. "Robert, allow me to introduce Sir Peter de Vere, knighted by our father on the field of battle, and appointed my personal bodyguard when I was sent to Germany to marry the Holy Roman Emperor."

Earl Robert was clearly taken aback, but he recovered swiftly and made a stiff bow.

"Sir Peter," he said.

Brother Peter bowed in return. He turned to Matilda.

"I thank you for your courtesy, my lady, but plain Brother Peter is all the title I would require of anyone now."

"It seems I have two brothers then," the Empress laughed, "brother Robert and Brother Peter. Let's sit down together then as we're a family!"

Earl Robert joined us, and his sister poured him a goblet of wine. He seemed a little happier now he knew how she came to treat a poor monk with such familiarity. I was astonished. I looked at Brother Peter and caught his eyes for a moment. He gave me a half-smile and looked away quickly as if he were embarrassed.

"Peter," the Empress said, and her voice had a seriousness in it that I hadn't heard before, "things really are not going well for me at all. When I had Stephen locked up two years ago and marched to London, I might have been crowned, but the people turned against me. Perhaps I was too high-handed with them." She looked away and watched her camp going about its business for a few moments. "They'd have taken it from a man," she said at last, "but not from a woman - not in this country." Her green eyes blazed up suddenly and she slapped her thigh. "It makes me mad," she cried. "If

Mary can be Mother of God, why can't Matilda be Mother of England?"

"Not for lack of courage, my lady," the Earl said, quietly.

"To be sure, Robert. It takes courage to be a mother."

"I meant the courage you've shown in this war," he said.

To my amazement, she looked down with an expression of shy pleasure like Arlette when sometimes my father would compliment her on her hair or a dress she was wearing.

"I don't know what you could possibly mean, my lord," she said.

"No man on earth can hold our sovereign captive," he said with force and pride. He looked from Peter to me and back again as he explained with mounting excitement how Matilda had been besieged at Oxford only a few weeks before and had escaped with a handful of knights by being let down from the castle walls on ropes during the night. They'd apparently walked across snow-covered fields and a frozen river, wrapped in white sheets, and crept straight through Count Stephen's army lines to freedom.

Peter rocked with laughter.

"You always were a wild girl," he said. He looked at Earl Robert, and it was clear that the two of them had found a bond in their admiration for this extraordinary woman. "You've no idea what a hard time she gave me – imagine trying to be a bodyguard to someone who does things like that!"

Matilda suddenly lurched forward and grabbed my friend's hand.

"Peter, Peter," she said excitedly, "do you remember that game I used to play with you? 'What would you do if...?'"

"How could I forget!"

She turned to Earl Robert and to me.

"I used to plague him constantly by making up disastrous situations and asking him what he'd do to get out of them. 'What would you do if...?' And he always came up with something."

"Whether they'd have worked..." Peter said.

"That's just it," she said. "One of them did! Do you remember once I said, 'What would you do if... you lost a battle and needed to escape?' Do you remember what you said?"

Brother Peter's round face puckered up in thought.

"It's a long time ago."

"Twenty-five years ago – I wasn't much older than monk cub here. Come on, Peter – you must remember. It had something to do with all the dead bodies!"

Peter jerked his head and laughed, beaming.

"I've got it!" he said. "I said I'd lie down on one of the carts taking the bodies away and pretend I was a corpse until they'd trundled me off the battlefield. Then I'd slide down and make a run for it. Stupid idea!"

"It wasn't," she laughed. "I did it, and it worked!"

"She did!" Earl Robert crowed. "I told you, no one in England can keep hold of her!"

"You saved me, baldy!" she said. "Still my bodyguard after all these years!"

We all laughed, but then she became suddenly serious.

"Be my bodyguard again," she said, earnestly. "I need you, Peter. I'm badly in need of generals who know their business and people I can trust." She turned to Earl Robert with the first kindly look I'd seen her give him. "I'm unfair to you Robert. I know it. You're a good and loyal friend, and a good soldier, and I do trust you. But there are not many like you." She turned to Peter again. "We will only win this war by courage and cunning," she told him, "and you're the bravest, cleverest champion I've ever known. What do you say?"

The Empress had captivated me and for the moment, I completely forgot that I had deep cause for loyalty to King Stephen. I longed for Brother Peter to say "yes", throw off his habit, strap on a sword belt, take me as his squire, and sign us up for her army. However, I didn't expect him to do it for one moment, so I was stunned when he put his hand to his head and seemed to be giving the offer serious consideration.

When she saw him wavering, Matilda turned to her brother for support.

"Robert? What do you say?"

The Earl became very formal.

"Sir Peter, I regret my earlier lack of courtesy. Our sovereign lady speaks the truth. We are in desperate need and would be much blessed by your assistance. England would be much blessed if you would join us."

"*Brother* Peter," my friend muttered, but he didn't meet Earl Robert's eyes. He still had his head in his hands.

It was several moments before Peter looked up. His big, strong face seemed vague and deeply troubled.

"My lady—" he began.

"Matilda - *your* Matilda," she insisted. "I need you, Peter. I really do. Please. Surely God has sent you to help me."

"Give me some time," Peter replied. "Meet your officers. Earl Robert is right - you must give the day's orders. Let me walk for a while, and then we'll speak again."

"Thank you, my friend," she said. "I'll take care of young John until you're ready."

"No, no," Peter told her. "I need John with me, if he'll come."

The thought of spending time in the royal tent was highly appealing, but when Peter stood, I stood with him and I followed as he walked away.

I had no idea what he wanted me for. Was I expected to say something? Advise him? I couldn't imagine what help I could be. But it turned out that nothing was required of me, other than to be at his side. I had assumed he would walk in the woods to do his thinking, but instead we wandered through the camp. The men were fully awake now, fed, and ready for whatever awaited them. Some were playing games with dice, or complicated boards with pegs and holes. Others were attending to equipment - cleaning and sharpening. In one area, pairs of men were practising with their swords and shields. Some of the soldiers looked at us strangely as we walked amongst them; others mumbled, "Morning, Father"; and a few asked us to pray for them or their families. Peter simply nodded. But when we came to the practice area, he asked for a sword. He swung it a few times, experimentally, then stepped forward and took on one of the men. He was offered a shield but refused, and he clearly didn't need it, as the other man never came near to hitting him. I was amazed at his skill. When he stepped away and returned the sword, there was a round of applause but he didn't acknowledge it. He walked slowly to the corral for the horses, where we'd spent the night. In daylight I could see that they were fine, well-groomed war horses, and Peter stayed some time there, stroking their necks, looking into their big eyes, and murmuring things to them. It was after this that he finally seemed to realise that I was there.

"Good," he said. "I'm ready."

And we walked back towards the royal tent.

"Why did you need me with you?" I asked, puzzled.

"Because God doesn't want us to face things alone," he said. "And because of all the things I've shared with you. You are all I have of my community, Brother John. St Mary's is one life. This is another. I needed to be close to them both - not to run away from either."

"What have you been doing as we walked?"

"Praying," he said. "What else should I do?"

When the Empress saw us approaching, she stopped one of her nobles in the middle of a sentence simply by raising her hand.

"One moment, my lord," she said.

They were meeting in the open in front of her tent, and she beckoned us inside.

"Well?" she said, eagerly.

"My lady—" Peter began.

She tutted and he tried again.

"Matilda," he said, "this kingdom - your kingdom - is being destroyed by infidelity. How can anyone put it right by breaking even more vows?"

"I don't understand you."

"The great men of England promised your father that you would be their monarch and they would serve you, and they have broken their word. I have promised my heavenly Father that he will be my monarch and I will serve him."

"Well serve him by serving me - serve truth and put the rightful monarch on the throne of England."

It seemed a good argument to me, but I could see that Peter was unmoved. The uncertainty had left his face.

"I have promised to serve in another army," he said. "St Mary's is my camp, and the Abbot is my commander."

"But, Brother Peter," I butted in.

They both turned to me.

"Your position at St Mary's..." I tailed off and hoped that Peter would catch my drift.

"Ah," he said, and turned back to the Empress. "There is a little difficulty at the moment. Only temporary, we hope. That was why John and I were wandering in the forest."

"They've thrown you out?" she asked, and despite the seriousness of the discussion, she couldn't help a snort of laughter. "What have you been up to, you old dog?"

"He's been up to nothing, my lady," I burst in. "We're trying to clear his name. He's been wrongly accused of theft."

"Well that *is* false," Matilda replied. "If Peter's ever stolen anything in his life, then I'm a bullfrog."

"What's happened doesn't release me from my vows, John," he told me. "It's like a marriage - sometimes there are problems, misunderstandings, even separations for a time, but the promises remain. You have to work to put things right, not give up and walk away."

Again, the Empress snorted.

"Has someone been telling you about *my* marriage?" she asked.

"That wasn't in my mind," he said with a smile.

The Empress turned to me.

"My husband the Emperor died when I was quite young, John, so my father packed me off to marry the Count of Anjou. He was only a year older than you when I married him - far too young for me, but these things can't be helped when marriages get mixed up with politics. People call him 'Geoffrey the Handsome'. He is, it's true, and he's given me three fine sons, but he is not an easy man to get along with. Still, as Peter says, promises are promises. He remains my husband. And I could certainly do with him here now, instead of marching his army round Normandy. I sent Robert to bring him over, but he still won't come."

She paused, and I wondered how easy she was herself to get along with in a marriage. Peter and the Empress were looking at each other steadily.

"I take it that you're turning me down then, Brother Peter," she said at last.

"With deep regret, my lady," he replied.

Remembering the swings of mood I'd already seen that morning, I wondered how she would take this, but something told me that there was a bond between them that was deeper than spats of bad temper. A moment later, one of her snorting laughs told me I was right.

"Well, I expect you're past it anyway," she said. "But what about the monk cub?"

She turned and bowed close to me.

"You've taken no vows, John," she said. "You'll soon be old enough to be a squire and I'm sure this war will last long enough for you to have your chance. Will you serve your sovereign?"

"I've said I'll help Brother Peter clear his name, my lady," I replied.

"Turned down by two men in one day!" she laughed.

"Besides, my lady," Brother Peter reminded her, "If John serves you he may have to face his father on the field of battle one day."

That thought brought the winter's chill to us all.

"True enough, old friend," she said. "There's enough of that as it is, in this war, without us adding to it."

She called for servants, and we were provided with as much food as Brother Peter was prepared to accept for the rest of our journey, and a detachment of soldiers was made ready to escort us safely out of the way of danger. When we parted, the Empress Matilda, Lady of the English, stooped a little and looked into my face. I have never seen anything like her eyes - so bright but so dangerous.

"Pray for me, John, and I will pray for your father," she said. "Pray that we never meet."

Chapter Twelve

Hearing voices

As dusk fell that evening, a day's walking separated us from Matilda's forces. Our escort had left us long ago, and the buildings of Far Grange were now in sight. Brother Peter was anxious for us not to be spotted so he beckoned me to join him in a drainage ditch, to wait there until the light was gone and we could creep the last half-mile to hide in one of the barns. Our day's journey had been largely silent, not really for fear of attracting attention - the countryside seemed completely deserted - but because our encounter with the Empress had left us speechless. Who could tell what feelings kept Brother Peter in brooding silence? For myself, I needed time to readjust my thoughts about my companion. So much fell into place now that I knew he had been a knight and one so good that a king would entrust him with the safety of his daughter. But there were many new questions now, and Brother Peter's deep silence didn't encourage me to ask them. Instead, I wove all kinds of fantasies about my friend and the Empress Matilda and the life they had known at the court of the Holy Roman Emperor.

It was cold and damp in the ditch. Brother Peter whispered that it would be quite some time before we could safely make our move. My bones ached and I was bored. It's one thing to follow your own thoughts as you stride along, with the physical effort to keep you warm and the sights and sounds of the winter world to keep you entertained; but a gradually freezing and stiffening body in a ditch needs distraction. At last, I was driven to speak.

"You must have been a good knight," I suggested.

"The best," he said, in a tone that lacked any hint of boasting.

"Have you been in many battles?"

"Enough for one lifetime."

"Did you have to fight to defend the Empress."

We were whispering, and Brother Peter had to struggle to contain a laugh.

"The only defence she needed was against herself," he said.

I didn't know how to raise the subject that had preoccupied me most during the day, but I had to try.

"You seem to like her a lot," I said.

"Those 14 years at the Emperor's court are one of the treasures of my life."

"Were you—" I struggled but I couldn't find any other way of saying it - "were you in love with her?"

Again he fought with laughter.

"You don't understand, John," he explained. "She was a child. I was her guardian more than her bodyguard when King Henry sent me with her to Germany. She was only 8 or 9 when we went to the Emperor's court. I had to look after her during the three years she was being trained to be an Emperor's consort. She was only 12 when she was married - younger than you. I loved her, John - but as a younger sister, and a friend, nothing else. She grew into a beautiful young woman before we parted, I wasn't blind to that, but there was never any romance. She was someone else's husband by then, after all."

"Then why did you give everything up and become a monk?"

"Ah," he said, "I see the story you've been weaving about me! It wasn't a broken heart that sent me into a monastery. A monastery is no place for people who are running away."

"Then what?"

"I'd sworn service to Matilda while she was at the Emperor's court, but when her husband died and she returned home to her father, King Henry, my duty was done. I had to decide whom to serve next. I could have returned with her to her father's court but 14 years at the centre of the Holy Roman Empire had spoiled me for that. The time with Matilda was a blessing, but not the politics - everyone binding and unbinding themselves to various lords, swapping allegiances whenever the wind of fortune changed. And the way noble children like Matilda were married off - used like pieces in a game to win more power. I wanted to serve something bigger - more faithful and honest than all of that. So I decided to become a knight of the King of Kings - if his generals would have me - and I became a novice in a monastery in France. That was nearly 20 years ago." He paused and shook his head in disbelief. "Bless me," he said, "I haven't seen the girl for almost 20 years."

It was almost dark, and I knew we would be moving soon.

"It was Matilda that taught me how to paint," Brother Peter added, after a silence. "She was good. Did you see how well her dress went with her hair? She always had an eye for colour."

* * *

After the cold, and the hard ground we'd slept on the previous night, the Grange barn seemed luxurious when we got inside. A man who had been bodyguard to an empress was not going to have any problem entering a farmyard barn undetected, and Brother Peter brought us to our hideaway without incident. It was a sturdy building, with thick walls to keep out the winter wind. And the grain sacks made much more warm and comfortable bedding than the frozen earth. We slept well and long, and it was a good job that Brother Peter had taken the precaution of making a den for us out of sight at the back of the barn, as we were awoken by the sound of voices. The barn doors were open, letting in hard, frosty sunlight, and two men were standing inside the building talking.

One of the voices in particular startled me out of my sleep. "The usual amount?" he said.

"I have Father Prior's authority," the other replied – presumably a lay brother. "I'm to supply the King's army as agreed. And Father Prior has sent more money for the King's cause."

"Most welcome," the man told him. "King Stephen has much need of money and corn at the present to pay his mercenaries and to feed them."

Brother Peter was awake and he put his arm around me to keep me from moving, but I was rigid and almost holding my breath.

"Father Prior is most anxious that his loyal love and greetings be carried to the King," the lay brother was saying.

The man heaved a weary sigh.

"You may assure the Prior that the King will reward the faithfulness he has shown. You may tell Father Prior that he can expect to sit in a bishop's throne and drink wine in a bishop's palace when the war is won."

More voices could then be heard, and the creaking of a cart being backed up to the barn doors. Brother Peter and I lay still as we listened to the grunting and muttering of several lay brothers loading corn onto a wagon. At last it was over. The heavy doors closed, and we were safe to speak.

"No wonder things went wrong once the Prior got to know the fraud in the monastery had been discovered," Brother Peter began. "It's obviously the Prior who planned it. He must have been using Brother Hubert as a go-between so that he could shift the blame. Hubert and the Prior are both from Boulogne and Stephen is Count of Boulogne. I should think if we could dig into it we'd find the Count or the Prior has some hold over Hubert or his family to stop him speaking out."

Peter punched a sack of corn.

"This corn is supposed to be for the starving poor," he said, angrily, "and instead it's being given to the soldiers who are making them starve. Stephen's been buying support from churchmen and nobles and merchants across the whole country. If ever he wins this war he'll find he owes so many favours that he'll never be able to govern. It's a disaster."

He stopped and seemed to realise that I was very still and quiet.

"Are you all right, boy?" he asked.

"That man getting the corn," I said. "I recognised his voice. It was my father."

My throat felt dry and my face was hot.

"How could he?" I said. "He's a knight. How can he steal - and from a monastery too?"

"Maybe he doesn't know," Brother Peter said, gently. "As far as he's concerned the whole monastery could be in agreement with this."

"Of course!" I cried. "He's been taken in like everyone else. And once he knows, he'll be so angry, he'll ride straight to St Mary's and tell the Abbot, and your name will be cleared."

I jumped up and headed for the door. Brother Peter made a grab for me and I heard him shouting, "John, no!" but I'd taken him by surprise again and scrambled out of our den before he could get a grip on me. I barged the huge wooden doors open and stood, blinking in the light. I saw various lay brothers turning towards the barn in astonishment, then I saw the loaded wagon and its armed escort making off down the track away from the Grange. Leading them was my father, bareheaded but in his battle-mail.

"Father!" I shouted at the top of my lungs, and sprinted after him.

I saw him swivel in the saddle, and I shouted again. He raised his hand to halt the wagon and when I shouted a third time he turned his horse and cantered towards me.

He reigned in beside me, slipped from his saddle and grasped me in a bear hug, saying was it really me, and how much he'd missed me. I was hugging him tightly, too, and strangely it felt as if he were hanging on to me for support.

"You're so big!" he said, when he finally stood back from me and looked me up and down. "And you're looking so well - a diet of monk's bread and hard work must suit you."

I said nothing, but my thoughts on seeing my father after so long were almost the exact opposite. He looked tired, ill, and much smaller than I'd remembered him.

"Did your wounds mend?" I asked him.

"Oh yes, John - long ago," he said. "I've had one or two more since then, but none so bad." He looked up, past my shoulder. "And none cared for as well as at St Mary's," he said.

I turned and saw Brother Peter walking towards us.

"I think I owe you my life, Brother," my father said.

"You remember me then?" Brother Peter replied.

"Once seen, never forgotten."

"You owe your son as much as you owe me. He got you to our valley."

"True enough," my father said, and put his arm round my shoulders.

Again, I felt the weight of him bearing down on me. We were silent for a long moment, then one of his men's horses snorted and stamped and he looked round almost as if he'd forgotten they were there. He gave them an order to dismount and asked me what I was doing at Far Grange.

"It's dangerous to be travelling," he said. "You must have passed close to the Countess of Anjou's forces."

"The Empress Matilda, you mean?"

"She's the Countess of Anjou, John, nothing more," he told me, and there was the same weariness in his voice as when he'd told the lay brother that the Prior would get his reward. It felt as if he were reading out some dull proclamation that he'd read a dozen times before.

"You know where she is then?" I asked.

"She's travelling with a small force to rejoin her main army. We've been playing hide and seek across the country with her for weeks," he said. "She's somewhere near about - too near for you to be travelling safely outside St Mary's."

I wondered whether it was my duty to tell my father of our encounter in the forest. But I was no longer sure what duties I had to anyone. All I knew was that I had to clear Brother Peter's name and disentangle my father from the crime he was unwittingly involved with.

"Father," I said. "I have something very important to tell you. You've been badly deceived. Your honour is in danger."

A few minutes later, Father, Brother Peter and I were sitting in a small private parlour in the Grange. I had told my story, and now there was a silence so heavy that it seemed to be pressing down on my shoulders. Brother Peter had said nothing, but I knew that for some reason he was deeply uneasy with what I was doing. My father had not spoken, either, as I had given him the details. Now, he was staring at the stone-flagged floor. I looked quickly at Brother Peter. He too had bowed his head.

Without looking up, my father said, "Would you leave us, please, Brother?"

Brother Peter glanced at me, but I could read nothing but uncertainty in his expression. He walked out without a word.

When he had gone, I expected my father to look up, but he scraped the stones with his foot and didn't meet my eyes.

"John," he said at last, "war is a mess. It's a mess from start to finish. I've seen things that will give me nightmares for the rest of my life. There's precious little honour in any of it - except in doing your duty perhaps."

"But there's honour here," I said. "You can clear Brother Peter's name and your honour."

There was a long pause.

"Son, I already knew," he said, looking up at last.

"What?"

I couldn't for the moment understand what he meant.

"I knew how the money was got. I know the corn is being taken without proper permission."

At that moment I felt that there was nothing worse that could happen to me in the whole world. It felt as if my father were disappearing in front of my eyes, leaving nothing but a talking shadow.

"Then why are you doing it?" I asked - desperate for some explanation that would bring him back before he disappeared completely.

"It's my duty, John. The King's orders. Baron Gilbert's orders. This is Baron Gilbert's land after all. It's my money that helped build the monastery. We've a right to expect something back now, when the King needs it."

"But it's *not* yours," I protested. "Baron Gilbert gave the land. You gave the money. You can't give something then take it back."

"We're not taking it back - we're *expecting* something back."

"Then you should ask properly," I said, and I suddenly realised there were tears in my eyes. "You should ask the Abbot and Chapter to agree - not just sneak things out. Look what it's led to. Brother Peter's in disgrace - he's going to be thrown out of the monastery."

"They wouldn't agree, John. Surely you've been there long enough to know that."

"Then you have no right to take the things."

"It's not me that's taking them!" My father sounded as desperate as me. We were like two boys arguing about the rights and wrongs of some squabble over toys. "It's the *King*."

"The Count of Boulogne," I corrected.

He stared at me in confusion.

"I have to do my duty," he repeated. "It's a knight's duty to serve his lord and follow his lord's orders."

"Is it a knight's duty to steal?" I asked.

His head sank. I couldn't believe that I'd just said the things I'd said to my father. But then he no longer felt like my father. I suddenly realised that it had been so long since I'd seen him that I'd built up a fantasy in my head and that had become more real than the flesh and blood. We'd both been changed by time and I realised that I didn't really know this stooped figure, staring at his feet. But I did know that I loved him and needed him as much as I'd loved and needed the bleeding knight, dying in my arms almost two years ago. I felt very lonely and frightened.

"Father, don't leave me," I said. "You promised."

He looked up and his eyes were red.

"What do you mean, son?" he asked.

"Don't stop being you," I said.

He put his arms out to me and I knelt clumsily on the floor in front of him so that we could clasp each other tight.

"I don't know what to do," he murmured, and his voice was thick with tears.

Neither did I. We held each other for a long time. And I prayed - not a long or fancy prayer - just three simple words, "God help us." And then, suddenly, I knew what to do.

"Let's talk to Brother Peter," I said.

Slowly we released each other.

"He's just a monk," my father said. "What would he know about it?"

"He's not just a monk," I said. "He used to be a knight like you. He served King Henry. He knows all about how difficult things can be. He's told me."

My father thought for a long time.

"Fetch him," he said, at last.

By the time I got back to the parlour with Brother Peter, my father seemed to have recovered a little from the emotions we'd shared. He was sitting up straight and his face looked stern.

"This will be a strange confession, Brother Peter," he said, as my friend sat down. "I don't imagine it's usual to have a third party present. But I suppose we're all in this together."

Brother Peter returned my father's stern stare and waited.

"You are in Holy Orders, I take it?" my father asked.

"I am, Sir Henry."

"Then please take what passes between us in the spirit of the confessional. I am aware that your good name is at issue here, and your future at St Mary's, but can you put that aside and speak to me simply as a priest - and as a priest who once, I understand, was a knight?"

"With the help of God, I will," Brother Peter replied.

With this assurance, my father told him what he had told me.

"So, Brother, what do you make of it? If you can speak to me as a priest and not a man on the run, tell me what I should do. What would you do?"

Brother Peter waited a moment. His eyes were closed. Perhaps he was praying. Then he looked at my father with great compassion.

"What would I do?" he said. "I can tell you I have already done much that required confession."

I must have gasped, because Brother Peter turned to look at me. It was the first time that either of them had acknowledged that there was a witness to this exchange.

"Yes, John," he said. "This is not a world of perfect people, anywhere - you must know that by now." He addressed my father again. "As for what you should do, Sir Henry, I think you must find that out for yourself. But it may help to think about this - what would you do if Baron Gilbert, the lord to whom you have promised service, asked you to do something and then King Stephen commanded you not to do it?"

"I wouldn't do it," my father answered, without hesitation.

"Because?"

"Because each baron is sworn to serve the King, so anything the King commands must become the will of the baron."

"Or should, at any rate. So, now, tell me, whom is every Christian monarch sworn to serve?"

"Their people and their God," my father replied.

"Exactly," Brother Peter told him. "So, as Christian knights, our service is promised to our lord, and through our lord to our monarch, and through our monarch to our God. And when orders contradict each other, we must go to the highest authority. So the only real question here is: what does God command?"

There was a small chapel attached to the Grange, so that worship could continue even in this distant branch of the monastery. Brother Peter suggested that the three of us went there to pray silently for God's help in our troubles. We knelt for some time, until my knees were aching. I wasn't aware of praying in words. I just pictured my father's poor, distressed face and his red-rimmed eyes, and held the image there in my heart and mind in the presence of God. At last there was a movement. I opened my eyes a little and saw that my father was leaving. I started to get up, but Brother Peter put his hand on my arm and the two of us stayed where we were. I found that now it was my friend's round face that I pictured, framed by his monk's hood.

When Brother Peter finally nudged me to get up, my knees were so numb that he had to help me to my feet. When we got outside, we saw the detachment of soldiers still standing guard over the wagon of corn. Brother Peter called out to them to ask where Sir Henry was and they said he had gone into the Grange, calling for vellum and a quill. My father came out a few moments later holding the vellum and marched up to us holding it out in front of him.

"Take this," he said, giving it to Brother Peter. "I hope it may be of some use. Read it, John."

I stood next to Brother Peter and read, in my father's big, clumsy writing, a letter of thanks to the Abbot and Chapter of St Mary's for the donations of money and provisions which the Prior had so kindly organised to be sent to the King's army.

"Forgive me for not being perfect," my father said to me, quietly, "but I promised never to leave you, and if I return the corn and the money, I'm afraid I might well have to break that promise."

As he rode away with his soldiers, I asked Brother Peter what he had meant.

"Serving a lord can be costly, John," he explained. "Any knight knows he may have to give his life in battle. Serving the Lord God is no different. If Sir Henry were to return without the corn and money that the King is expecting, he might well lose his head - and you would lose your father. This way, when we take his letter back with us, my name will be cleared and the supply of money and corn will be stopped for the future. God answers prayer in interesting ways."

* * *

I'd like to be able to write down how this story ends. But I can't, because it hasn't ended yet - my story, the story of the war, the story of Brother Peter and St Mary in the Wilds. The war goes on. The life of the world goes on. The seasons have turned and it's summer now at St Mary's. The crops are ripening. Plenty of food for the poor - those who survived the winter. And much more of it will be going where it's supposed to go this year. My father's letter did its work. Brother Peter is back where he belongs - painting, ploughing and praising God. The Prior and Brother Hubert were expelled from the monastery, but word has reached us that King Stephen makes use of them still. They preach the King's cause in churches and at market crosses where Stephen has support, gathering ever more money to pay his mercenaries and bribe the powerful people of the land. Brother Peter says they're destined for greatness in this kingdom, if not in the kingdom of heaven.

And I have spent six months writing all this down, as the sun gradually thawed the land and brought deep green back to our pastures. I've written it because I need to understand things and make a decision. The Abbot spent a long time with me after Brother Peter and I returned with Father's letter. He praised me for what I had done, and he was angry in a way I'd not seen before when he spoke about the Prior and his accomplice.

"Even here, we can't escape the temptations of wealth and power!" he said, gripping his hands into fists as if he wanted to punch someone, or something. "We can't escape our humanity, I suppose," he said. He was quiet for a while after that, until he had control of himself again. Then he said that he needed to speak to me about my future. He told me that I couldn't stay as I was at St Mary's forever. My position at the monastery had always been highly irregular - not a novice, not a lay brother. "But then, you were only a boy," he explained, "and as we have never had children at St Mary's, we had no arrangements to guide us. That didn't seem to matter, to begin with. But we none of us had any idea how long this war would drag on - how long you would be with us. A few months could be overlooked - but months are becoming years now. You will not be a boy much longer, John. There will come a time when a decision must be made – whether you have a vocation to the life of a monk, or whether you should perhaps join the lay brothers at Far Grange. Or perhaps your father will want to take you into his service."

The Abbot didn't say when I must decide, and he hasn't spoken to me again about it. But I know that he's right. I must make up my mind. I think I knew that before my conversation with the Abbot. I knew it the moment that the Lady Matilda asked me to be her squire. I could never serve her while my father served King Stephen, but I could become a squire – my father's squire. A way was open – a possibility of leaving this place. My father could hardly complain of the danger – even some monasteries have now been attacked, we hear. So the months have passed and I have written everything down to help me see clearly what I should do. Now it is finished. These are the final pages, and I'm no nearer to knowing. What comes next? I suppose I'll simply put this under my mattress and keep on ploughing, and painting. Brother Peter says I'm almost as good a painter as the Empress, when she was my age. And I'll keep on praising God, too, in my own way, for what he has done and is doing in my life.

I once asked Brother Peter, after our winter adventure, why he'd come back to England. He became a monk in France, so why didn't he stay there?

"Who knows?" he said. "Monks were needed to start a new house in England and the Abbot asked me to be one of them. He knew I'd been a soldier - perhaps he thought I'd have the skills to hack a camp out of the wilderness and survive. But there were other ex-soldiers he could have asked. Perhaps I came here to help save your father's life and teach you to paint."

When we had this conversation, we were tending sheep near to the place where Father and I had come out of the forest that day two years ago, his life blood draining away, and me thinking my world was coming to an end. Ridiculous thoughts started to form in my mind. Had my father been drawn to give money to the monastery so that one day he would be able to come here when he needed healing - so that one day his son could spend two years growing up here? Did everything that happened somehow fit into some great big story that no one could ever know the whole of? How could such a thing be organised? It was beyond all sense or reason.

But those thoughts have stayed with me as I've been writing this down - my little bit of the story. They still seem ridiculous to my head, but not to my heart. Somehow in this land of broken vows it feels deep inside me as if there is one promise that stays true - the promise that everything is being held in some great story and that the storyteller will never abandon any of the characters. They are all watched over and not one of them is lost. They all have their part to play. But what my part is going to be, I still don't know. When I discuss these things with Brother Peter he tells me I need to wait patiently - to keep on ploughing and painting and praying, and listen to my heart. So that's what I'll do, I suppose. It's time for the afternoon office now. I can hear the bell. So I'll put this away and go to church. And in a little while I'll get out into God's good air, enjoy the sun as it ripens the corn, and listen to my heart.

Historical note

Matilda never did gain the crown that the barons of England had promised she should have. But King Stephen agreed that on his death Matilda's son Henry should be the next King of England. So eventually the years of chaos and civil war that are known in English history as "The Anarchy" came to an end. The promise about Matilda's son was kept, and when King Stephen died in 1154 the young man was crowned Henry II of England. One of his nicknames was "FitzEmpress" - son of the Empress. He also came to rule vast areas of France - establishing a secure reign over more of Europe than any English monarch before or since. His son was Richard the Lionheart and the ruling dynasty that Henry "FitzEmpress" founded - the Plantagenets - became the longest-lasting royal house in English history, reigning for over 300 years. All these kings and queens are long gone now, of course, and the Plantagenets, for all their centuries of power, are just a page in history. But the Lord whom Brother Peter vowed to serve is reigning still, and always has, and always will.

Want a sneak preview of another *Lifepath Adventure*?
Read on for the first chapter of

Hard Rock

Chapter 1

The bed rocked as a strong hand shook Collan awake.

"On your feet, then, if you want to join the hard rock men."

He screwed his eyes shut, then forced them open. In the half-light, his older brother Jem was grinning down at him.

Collan stared up at him. Then he was out of bed with one bound as the truth struck home.

It was his twelfth birthday. He was going underground to work as a miner.

He scrabbled to pull on his clothes. He'd been working at Wheal Courage since he was 8, but always "above grass". Until today.

He scurried down the ladder from the wooden platform where the children slept. Behind him, the little ones, Mary and Dick, were still making sleepy moans under the blankets. But Collan couldn't wait.

His mother smiled at him and thrust a steaming mug into his hand. He took a gulp.

"Tea! Real tea? Not nettle brew?"

"'Tis a special day, isn't it? The first day you go below grass."

There was a hunk of bread. The fire of furze spat golden sparks. He looked up to find his father and Jem with broad smiles on their faces. Father drew something out from behind his back. It was bulky and round, wrapped in the sort of grey paper bag his mother bought sugar in, when she could afford it.

"Happy birthday, boy."

Collan began to guess what it was, even as his fingers were pulling the string from the paper. But he hardly dared to hope. The wrapping fell away.

He was holding in his hands his own tinner's hat. It was made of felt, soaked and squeezed and dried until it was as hard as wood. It had a narrow brim around it.

"Put it on," urged his big sister Kezia. "Let's have a look at you."

Collan set it on his head. It felt strange and hard, after the soft woollen cap he was used to. But he didn't care. He was one of them. He was going underground to mine copper and tin with his father and Jem.

His mother and Kezia had another parcel.

"Open it when you get there," Kezia said.

At the last moment, his mother hugged him fiercely.

"God be with you, child."

She didn't usually do that. A finger of fear touched Collan's heart. Mining was dangerous. The village had many men with broken bodies or ruined lungs. The churchyard held more.

***

The three of them set out in the early autumn morning. The sky over Cornwall was pale, the birds beginning to sing, but the sun was not up yet. Smoke was climbing all around them. It rose from the cottages they passed, from the tall chimneys of the blowing houses, where they smelted the tin. There was the sour tang of sulphur in the air.

It was a three-mile walk to Wheal Courage. All along the way, people were streaming towards the mine. Men whose hobnailed boots struck sparks on the stones. The bal-maidens in their white aprons and big bonnets. They were the women and girls who spent their days crushing and sorting the ore above grass. Children smaller than Collan came sleepily with them.

As they walked, someone began to sing. It was like this every morning. The Cornish tinners loved to sing as they walked and worked. A voice struck up Collan's favourite.

"And shall Trelawney die?
And shall Trelawney die?
Then thirty thousand Cornish boys
Will know the reason why."

That was a good one to put a swing in your stride.

The pump gear of the mine was looming nearer. The tension was tightening in Collan's chest.

Presently, when there was a lull in the singing, Collan's father started a new one.

"Jesu, lover of my soul,
Let me to thy bosom fly,
While the nearer waters roll,
While the tempest still is nigh."

It was a strong tune in Father's deep voice. Collan thought he had heard the grown-ups singing it at home. He didn't know the words. Nor, it seemed, did most people. Jem did, though. He sang along lustily with Father and a handful of others.

"That's a good 'un," one of the men called out. "Where did you pick that up?"

"It's one of Mr Charles Wesley's. A new one. He's not such a preacher as his brother John, but he's a wonderful gift with songs," said Collan's father. He began to sing again in his bass voice.

"Other refuge have I none,
Hangs my helpless soul on thee."

The other miners listened as they walked. By the time Father and Jem had reached the next verse, they started humming along. In the wonderful way the Cornish had, their voices were weaving the harmony. The men sang bass and tenor, with the bal-maidens picking up soprano and contralto. Collan's voice hadn't broken. He sang the melody with the trebles.

"Raise the fallen, cheer the faint,
Heal the sick, and lead the blind."

They sang to a rousing finish.

"Cheer the faint," thought Collan. "That's me this morning. I'm scared."

In the silence behind them, a lone girl's voice piped up a different tune.

"Charles Wesley is come to town
To try to pull the churches down."

There was a burst of laughter.

Collan's father rounded on her. Ned Retallick was not a big man, but he could look big when he was roused.

Facing him was a skinny girl with a freckled face, under the curve of the cardboard brim of her bonnet. Collan had a glimpse of ginger hair.

"You can keep a civil tongue in your head, Emblen Kitto. Your family would be a sight better off if your father paid heed to what the Wesleys say, and spent his wages on his children, and not at the ale house."

When he turned his back, the freckled girl stuck out her tongue at him.

***

They had almost reached the mine. Now that it was close, excitement was rising in Collan's throat, threatening to choke him. Not just excitement. There was dread too. He'd never been down the mine until today.

All around the shaft, workers were busy. The bal-maidens had changed the clean white aprons they wore to walk to the mine for brown sackcloth ones, stained with red. They were gathering in a chattering flock on the dressing floor, ready to attack the pile of rocks with their hammers.

Collan passed the horse-pump, where he had worked until yesterday. This morning, another boy was leading the horse in a circle, while the rope wrapped itself around a great wooden drum. It was hauling buckets up from underground. All day, every day, they had to pump the water out, to stop it flooding the mine.

Today, Collan was not a pump boy. He was beginning a man's work.

Still, he stopped for a moment to stroke Beauty, the sturdy brown horse. They had worked well together.

His father took him into a shed, where they stripped off their shirts and jackets. In Mother and Kezia's parcel was a sacking tunic. It was like the ones Father and Jem were slipping on. Only his was new and clean, while theirs were streaked red from the copper ore.

Jem set the tinner's hat on Collan's head. He took a lump of clay and stuck a new candle through it. Then he clamped it on Collan's helmet. Father hung a bundle of spare candles from the neck of his tunic. They both stepped back to admire their work.

"You'll do, boy," said Father.

They came out of the shed. Collan's bare arms struck chilly in the early morning air. It felt strange to be so lightly dressed. He gave a little shiver.

"Don't worry," laughed Jem. "It'll be hot enough where we're going."

The mouth of the shaft was steaming when Collan stood in front of it. The stink of sulphur was stronger. Collan swallowed a lump in his throat. He could see just the first rungs of the ladder.

Without warning, the sun burst up over the horizon in front of him. The dewdrops sparkled like jewels on the few patches of grass that hadn't been trampled. Columns of smoke from a multitude of chimneys striped the blue sky. Over on the dressing floor the bal-maidens were singing as they set to work.

"Take a last look at it, boy," said Father. "It'll be a good eight hours before you see daylight again."

When Collan looked down, his eyes were blinded by the sunrise. The deep shaft below him looked utterly dark.

"Ready?" asked Father.

Collan nodded.

More Lifepath Adventures!

Hard Rock

Fay Sampson

Collan can't wait to join his dad and brother as a Hard Rock man - a miner - but it doesn't take long for him to realise that the mine is a dangerous place. How will he cope having to work with his father's drunk workmate? And what difference will the visit of John Wesley make?

£4.99 978 184427 372 0

Pilgrim

Eleanor Watkins

Tom was all alone - what was he going to do? Then he remembered something his mother said. She said that if anything were to happen to her, he should go back to her home village of Scrooby, where good people, people called Separatists, would look after him. Should he join the Separatists - the Pilgrim Fathers - on their journey to the new world?

£4.99 978 184427 373 7

In the Shadow of Idris

Ruth Kirtley

Bryn can't make up his mind about Mary Jones. She doesn't go to church any more, and his mam says that Mary and her mum have started to follow the teachings of Outsiders. But to Bryn she seems normal and kind. What will Bryn do, though, when he finds out she's about to set out on a very dangerous road?

£4.99 978 184427 374 4

Want more action and adventure? Try these great books!

Look out for *The Lost Book Trilogy*, by Kathy Lee!

The Book of Secrets

Jamie and Rob live a simple life on the island of Insh More. But Rob dreams of more, and these dreams lead both of them into mortal danger. Will the book in the seal-skin bag help them?

£4.99 978 184427 342 3

The Book of Good and Evil

For Jamie, Rob and Ali, the magnificent island city of Embra holds different paths. Jamie struggles to make a living, and is constantly drawn to the book in the seal-skin bag. How will the words inside help him to cope with war, robbery and the treachery of Sir Kenneth?

£4.99 978 184427 368 3

The Book of Life

A blind beggar brings a mysterious message to the King of Lothian. An old friend needs your help... This is the start of a dangerous mission, taking Rob and Jamie far from Embra to a land of darkness, slavery and death. Will they ever be able to escape?

£4.99 978 184427 369 0

A Captive in Rome

Kathy Lee

"Where's Father?"

Conan, my brother, looked up the hill, where our dead and dying soldiers lay like fallen leaves... hundreds of them, too many to count. Faintly in the distance I heard the sound of a Roman trumpet.

A disastrous battle tears Brin's world apart. Captured and taken into slavery, he is forced to start a new life in the incredible city of Rome!

£4.99 978 184427 088 0

The Dangerous Road

Eleanor Watkins

Gwilym and his dog Brown are on their first trip taking his father's sheep to market. They'd be having a good time if Huw, the old shepherd, didn't always want to spoil their fun. But soon the dangers of the drovers' roads threaten to put a stop to their fun, and their lives altogether.

£4.99 978 184427 302 7

The Scarlet Cord

Hannah MacFarlane

Joshua is leading the Israelites towards the great city of Jericho. The army is getting ready to make its move. But on the plains in front of Jericho, four children are heading towards the greatest danger they have ever faced.

£4.99 978 184427 370 6

Fire by Night

Hannah MacFarlane

Moses is leading the Israelites out of Egypt, but for two members of the tribe of Asher, things have gone badly wrong.

£4.99 978 184427 323 2

Great books from Scripture Union

Fiction

Mista Rymz, Ruth Kirtley £3.99, 978 184427 163 4
Flexible Kid, Kay Kinnear £4.99, 978 184427 165 8
The Dangerous Road, Eleanor Watkins £4.99, 978 184427 302 7
Where Dolphins Race with Rainbows, Jean Cullop £4.99, 978 184427 383 5
A Captive in Rome, Kathy Lee £4.99, 978 184427 088 0
Fire By Night, Hannah MacFarlane £4.99, 978 184427 323 2
The Scarlet Cord, Hannah MacFarlane £4.99, 978 184427 370 6

The Lost Book Trilogy

The Book of Secrets, Kathy Lee £4.99, 978 184427 342 3
The Book of Good and Evil, Kathy Lee £4.99, 978 184427 368 3
The Book of Life, Kathy Lee £4.99, 978 184427 369 0

Fiction by Patricia St John

Rainbow Garden £4.99, 978 184427 300 3
Star of Light £4.99, 978 184427 296 9
The Mystery of Pheasant Cottage £4.99, 978 184427 296 9
The Tanglewoods' Secret £4.99, 978 184427 301 0
Treasures of the Snow £5.99, 978 184427 298 3
Where the River Begins £4.99, 978 184427 299 0

Bible and Prayer

The 10 Must Know Stories, Heather Butler £3.99, 978 184427 326 3
10 Rulz, Andy Bianchi £4.99, 978 184427 053 8
Parabulz, Andy Bianchi £4.99, 978 184427 227 3
Massive Prayer Adventure, Sarah Mayers £4.99, 978 184427 211 2

God and you!

No Girls Allowed, Darren Hill and Alex Taylor £4.99, 978 184427 209 9
Friends Forever, Mary Taylor £4.99, 978 184427 210 5

Puzzle books

Bible Codecrackers: Moses, Valerie Hornsby £3.99, 978 184427 181 8
Bible Codecrackers: Jesus, Gillian Ellis £3.99, 978 184427 207 5
Bible Codecrackers: Peter & Paul, Gillian Ellis £3.99, 978 184427 208 2

Available from your local Christian bookshop or from
Scripture Union Mail Order, PO Box 5148, Milton Keynes MLO, MK2 2YX
Tel: 0845 07 06 006 Website: www.scriptureunion.org.uk/shop
All prices correct at time of going to print.